To Lauren,

Enjoy the adventure...

Best wishes.

Secrets *of a* Christmas Box

On a quiet snowy street not that far from your own, is a house and a family's warm loving home. But unknown to them all lies a secret of old, that until this Christmas has never been told. So sit yourself down and snuggle up tight; there's more than meets the eye on this Christmas night.

Secrets of a
Christmas Box

STEVEN HORNBY

BOOKS

ECKY THUMP BOOKS
Glendale · California

SECRETS OF A CHRISTMAS BOX
AN ECKY THUMP BOOKS PUBLICATION

Text and illustrations copyright © 2009 Steven Hornby.

Edited by Judy Reveal and Golriz Fanai

Color illustration by Justin Gerard

Chapter illustrations by Gabriel Hordos

ISBN: 978-0-9815883-0-8

Library of Congress Control Number: 2008924155

FIRST EDITION

Printed in China
by Codra Enterprises, Inc

10 9 8 7 6 5 4 3 2 1   09 10 11 12 13 14 15

ECKY THUMP BOOKS, INC
P.O. Box 3524
Glendale, CA 91221-0524
USA

www.eckythumpbooks.com

To Mom & Dad

From the start of December,
to Christmas Eve night,
one chapter an evening,
wrapped up with delight.

Contents

*On a quiet snowy street
not that far from your own,
is a house and a family's
warm loving home.*

*But unknown to them all
lies a secret of old,
that until this Christmas
has never been told.*

*So sit yourself down
and snuggle up tight;
there's more than meets the eye
on this Christmas night.*

I

The Family Tree

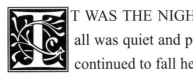T WAS THE NIGHT BEFORE CHRISTMAS EVE, and all was quiet and peaceful on Blenheim Drive. The snow continued to fall heavily, as it had done on and off for the past few days. Mr. Ferguson was returning home from an afternoon of last minute Christmas shopping with his two young children, Aaron and Emma. He drove slowly and carefully in the snow, finally turning the corner onto their street. The rows of elm trees that lined both sides of the street were bare of their leaves and the wet snow lay heavily on their branches, bending them towards one another across the street until it seemed that Mr. Ferguson was driving through a tunnel of ice. Aaron and Emma sat quietly in the back seats, staring out of the windows at the array of Christmas lights and decorations that twinkled through their neighborhood.

The car slid a little as Dad gently turned it into the driveway and stopped, illuminating the falling snow in front of the old brick house. Icicles large and small hung from the roof and window ledges. The large, dormant bushes in the front garden, grown from clippings taken from grandma's house many years ago, were now just a series of gentle bumps and mounds under the thickening white blanket.

Dad turned off the car engine just as the red door to the house opened wide and Mom appeared on the step, drying her hands on the kitchen towel. She had been baking most of the day and her apron was covered with flour. Emma and Aaron unbuckled their seat belts and jumped out of the car into the deep snow. They giggled to one another and ran up the snowy path to Mom.

"*Hey, Mom!*" called Aaron, trying to beat Emma to the door.

"Hi, kids!" smiled Mom as she looked at the large Christmas tree tied to the roof of the car. "So we *did* get a tree after all…"

"*Yeah! And it smells all piney-like too!*" giggled Aaron, quickly kissing her before running inside.

"So, did you both have a great time?"

"*Yeah…!*" clapped Emma, kissing Mom's warm cheek. "*It was great! We saw Santa's helpers and everything.*" She too ran inside into the warm hallway where her cold cheeks, fingers and ears immediately felt tingly from the sudden warmth.

Floating through the house was the unmistakable smell of fresh gingerbread cookies, mixed with the smell of cinnamon from the warm mulled wine that Mom had been busy preparing since early afternoon.

"Hey, you two!" smiled Mom, glancing back into the house. "What's your Dad told you both about taking your shoes off at the door?"

They sighed and looked under their shoes and around the wooden floor, to see if they had brought in any dirt or snow.

"Now come back here both of you, and get them off before your Dad finds out!"

They hastily ran back, quickly kicked off their shoes, hung up their coats and sped back towards the stairs.

"I'm getting it!" giggled Emma, trying to push her brother away into the living room.

"No you're not! I'm the oldest," insisted Aaron. "I'll get it. It's still going to be too heavy for you!"

"*Now you two!* Be careful up there," warned Mom, watching them scurry up the stairs. "Remember, it's fragile, so help one another bring it down... *You hear me?*" she called, as the two of them disappeared into the bedroom. "*Oh and don't forget...! Don't go rooting through anything else in there! Just get the box from on top of the bed. Okay...?*" She turned back around and noticed Dad struggling to slide the Christmas tree off the top of the car.

"Hi, love!" smiled Mom from the front doorstep. "Wow, it's a big one this year!"

"Yeah...! Only the best for this house!" said Dad, finally sliding it down onto the ground. He shook the snow from its branches, and had a closer look. "It was the last one too, so he let us have it half price," he said, smiling proudly.

"Are you sure we're going to get it inside?" asked Mom, who was beginning to look a little worried at how he would fit it through the front door.

"I guess there's only one way of finding out," laughed Dad,

and he carefully lifted the tree through the snow, up to the front door while trying his best not to slip in his shoes.

"Hi, love," smiled Dad as he arrived at the doorstep, and kissed her on the lips.

Mom stepped in from the doorway to give Dad some space, and watched him as he attempted to pull the tree in by its stump. He huffed and sighed as the larger branches slid and scraped along the edges of the door frame until finally, with an extra big tug, the tree squeezed through the door and into the warm house.

"Brrrrrr… Cripes, it's cold out there," said Dad, shivering as he closed the front door, then banged his shoes on the doormat to knock off the snow. "Ooh, my feet are killing me. Thank goodness all the Christmas shopping's finally done this year."

Mom smiled at the tree, watching the branches begin to open out, to show its natural splendor. Even before Dad could lift it across the room, the fresh smell of pine began to mix with the gingerbread and mulled wine, creating that unmistakable smell of Christmastime throughout the house.

Carrying the tree across the wooden floor, he set it down in the same place every other tree had spent Christmas since they moved into the house over ten years ago. The tree was standing safely away from the Victorian fireplace that warmed the charming room. Opened Christmas cards were perched on top of the wooden mantel above the Christmas stockings, waiting to be filled by Santa Claus.

Dad finally balanced the large bushy tree upright, after turning it a couple of times to makes sure the best side was facing out into the room. It was a very tall and proud tree, thick with branches and very, very green.

Dad stepped back and held Mom's hand as they listened to Christmas carols on the radio and admired the tree's beauty.

"Oops…!" freaked Dad, suddenly remembering something. He looked down under his shoes at the floor. "Ooh, that was lucky. Better get them off before the kids…!" He whipped off his shoes and threw them over to the door, a moment before the children clamored down the stairs. "Goodness me!" said Dad, smiling at Mom. "Now that was close!"

Aaron and Emma wrestled the large cardboard box all the way down the stairs. It had the words 'Christmas Box' elaborately printed on its lid and sides.

"*I got it!*" giggled Aaron, excitedly. He lifted the box from his sister's grasp and ran towards the tree. At seven years old, Aaron was a good two years older than his sister, and regularly took full advantage of that fact.

"No you didn't! You snatched it from me!" moaned Emma. "Mom, tell him to share it…!"

"Now come on you two, let's play gently," ordered Dad, trying to calm them both. "Remember, they're all very fragile, so you both need to be especially careful, okay!"

Aaron and Emma nodded back in silence.

Taking the box, Dad placed it down gently in front of the tree. "Now then, let's see what we have in here," said Dad. He gingerly lifted off the lid so everyone could look inside.

Emma was still a hair too short to see over into the box and tried peering in by pulling the side down with her hands.

Inside the box lay a huge array of tree decorations, Christmas lights and shiny strands of tinsel in green, red, silver and gold. Some decorations were still in their boxes, while others were just wrapped in their original tissue paper. Dad lifted out the Christmas lights, and began unraveling them from around a tatty piece of cardboard.

Aaron and Emma, both hoping to find their favorite decorations, delved eagerly into the box. "No!" gasped Aaron, stopping suddenly.

"What's the matter…?" asked Mom, as Emma lifted Aaron's elbow out of the box to see what he was holding.

"Look…!" sighed Aaron, and held up a broken ornament in his hand. He stared blankly at Mom wondering what to do next, then sniffed from his reddened nose, which was still cold from them being out in the snow earlier.

"Now be careful you two," warned Mom, gently lifting their hands out of the box. She knew some of the decorations were made of glass and their fingers could easily get cut on the sharp edges.

Aaron and Emma just stared quietly, watching Mom carefully remove the broken pieces from the box and take them safely through to the kitchen. "Okay… So who's up for milk and gingerbread cookies?" smiled Mom, trying to make light of the situation.

"Yes please... Yeah...!" clapped Aaron and Emma, jumping up and down, as Dad continued dressing the tree with lights.

Aaron and Emma looked back in the box in search of their favorite characters from last year. They were still bickering and pushing one another in an attempt to be the first to find them.

"Hey, I found him...!" announced Aaron. Emma stopped and pouted with her rosy red face.

Aaron quickly and carefully lifted out the ornament in eager anticipation, but to his shock it was only the top half of it. He frowned back into the box to see the rest lying there in pieces. "Not this one too...! Dad!" he sighed, looking up. Dad was inside the tree branches, blissfully whistling along to the carols on the radio.

"Dad! Look...! This one's the same...!" repeated Aaron.

Dad was so eager to finish the lights before anyone began hanging the tree ornaments up, that he did not want to come away from the tree just yet. "Don't worry son, just leave it to the side there and your Mom and I'll sort it out afterwards. Just be careful with it."

"This one's still okay though!" giggled Emma, pulling out a complete ornament.

Aaron dropped what he was holding back into the box and attempted to snatch the one she had in her hands. "No... Give it to me...!" snapped Aaron.

"No... I found it..." insisted Emma, struggling to keep it from Aaron. *"Dad! He's doing it again!"*

Dad poked his head out from behind the tree. "Don't make me come over there you two," he warned. "If you can't play nicely, you won't get any milk and cookies."

"But more importantly," said Mom, arriving back in from the kitchen, holding the tray of drinks and fresh cookies, "you both know, don't you!"

"No..." paused Aaron.

"All the decorations on the tree know Santa Claus *personally*," explained Mom, placing the tray down on the coffee table, next to a bowl of fresh nuts and tangerines. "So if you break one of them by snatching it from one another, then Santa's not going to be very happy with you now, is he?"

"Is that true…?" asked Dad, and noticed Mom looking over in astonishment at his question. He smiled with a wink, then glanced back at the children who were staring at Mom with their mouths wide open. They were both amazed that the tree decorations knew the magical man and immediately calmed down. The last thing they wanted to do was to upset Santa Claus so close to Christmas, especially when they had been so good all year.

Mom passed them each a glass of milk and extra large cookies. Dad had finished putting up the lights and was rewarded with a warm glass of mulled wine.

While Dad whistled along to the Christmas carols on the radio, they all helped empty out the Christmas box. The children were finally helping one another fill the tree with the wonderful decorations, while taking little breaks in between to finish off their milk and cookies. Mom and Dad were now relaxing after such a hectic day and enjoyed sipping on their mulled wine.

"Wow, look at this one!" exclaimed Dad, lifting a metal wind-up toy from the box. It was showing its age, since some of the paint had chipped off its body, and its string was looking rather frayed. "I was given this by my great grandmother," continued Dad nostalgically, "when she came back from mainland Europe…" He then passed it gently to Emma, who hung it up carefully with the rest of the ornaments.

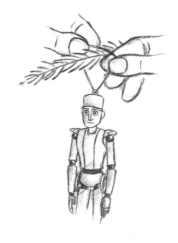

II

The New Addition

 HE FAMILY CONTINUED DRESSING THE TREE, filling it with the wonderful assortment of Christmas decorations from the Christmas box.

"Oh, I almost forgot," said Mom, quickly putting down her glass. "Here you go kids, something for you both!" and reached into her handbag, lying at the side of one of the couches.

Mom passed them something wrapped in white tissue paper. They hastily unwrapped it to reveal a shiny wooden character with rotating joints in its elbows and knees. Their eyes lit up and they eagerly added it to the tree, along with the other ornaments that now crowded the dense branches.

"I found it at the corner store on Lytham Road," explained Mom. "It was the last one left and I thought it would look good on the tree with everything else."

Dad nodded in agreement.

"So, when did you tell them we were getting a tree?" asked Mom.

"Yes, about that…" puzzled Dad. "They seemed to already know… It was as though, they'd already *been in the bedroom*, and seen the Christmas box on the bed… But I thought to myself… *No…!*" He held back a smile and glanced over to Aaron and Emma for a reaction. "They wouldn't go in the bedroom. They know better than that!"

The children pretended not to hear what Dad said; having been found out about sneaking into their parents' room, they were not going to give themselves away and admit to it.

Mom and Dad smiled at one another, knowing kids were just kids, especially at this time of year.

"Oh, by the way love," remembered Dad. "Are Alec and Doreen okay for looking after the cat?"

"Misty! Oh dear…" sighed Mom, looking outside the living room window into the falling snow. "I knew there was something I forgot to do!"

"I'm sure it'll be fine," smiled Dad, sipping his wine, "but we better ask today. We're going away on the twenty-seventh, which is only four days away."

"Yes, that's right," said Mom, refilling Dad's glass with warm wine. "Wow, that is short notice. I remember their car being in their driveway earlier, so I'll drop around in a minute and ask," then smiled. "I'm sure it'll be fine."

"So have we all finished then, kids…?" asked Dad, clapping

his hands together and rubbing them in anticipation of switching on the lights.

"Yeah, we're done! Can I switch the lights on this year?" asked Aaron hopefully.

"Sorry son, not this year. Maybe when you're a bit older," answered Dad, checking the wiring on the branches. "Okay! Let's plug it in then, shall we?" and bent down behind the tree to find the wall switch.

"Ready then?" asked Dad, with his fingers eager to flick the wall switch. "Drum roll please!" Aaron and Emma stepped close to Mom, who put her arms around them both, waiting for the finale.

A *'click'* and a flicker later, the lights illuminated into a dazzling display of white; magically lighting up the whole room. The children jumped up and down yelling excitedly.

Dad joined the family in looking admiringly at their beautiful tree. "Great work on decorating the tree, kids," acknowledged Dad, pulling his family in close. "I think it's the best looking tree we've ever had... Don't you think?"

Mom smiled at him, knowing she had heard him say the same thing every other Christmas, making it a part of the Christmas tradition in the Ferguson household.

"*Yeah...!*" giggled Emma, her face beaming with joy at the glistening tree.

"Now, who's ready for some roast beef and Yorkshire pudding then...?" asked Mom. "And then it's... *trifle!*"

"*Me... Me!*" replied Aaron, and they retreated to the kitchen. All except Emma that is, who remained in the living room, admiring the brightly twinkling lights and decorations that hung from the proud Christmas tree. She was utterly transfixed by its beauty and absolutely loved the magical time of year it represented.

"Come on, Emma… It'll still be there after dinner…!" called Dad from the kitchen. "And have you both washed your hands?" Emma looked to check, then wiped them quickly on her dress and ran through into the kitchen, leaving the tree in peace.

After dinner Mom and Dad were busy washing up the dirty pots in the kitchen and Aaron and Emma were in the warm living room, watching the end of a Christmas cartoon on the television. The room felt very special with the tree shining out into it, especially with the smell of pine, gingerbread and roast beef from dinner still wafting around in the air. Emma was curled up on the couch, sucking her thumb. She kept glancing at the tree, then swinging her knees together excitedly. Meanwhile, Aaron was flat out on his belly in front of the television, drawing the Christmas tree in his sketchpad with the assortment of colored crayons that were scattered on the floor around him.

"Okay! It's time for bed, kids!" called Mom and Dad, walking in from the kitchen. Aaron and Emma pretended not to hear the phrase they had come to dread at nighttime.

"Come on both of you. Chop-Chop! You know it's bath night tonight," clapped Dad, "and if we have it tonight… What does that mean…?"

They both sighed.

Emma dropped off the couch, Aaron got up off the floor and

they dragged themselves slowly towards the hallway door.

"Yeah. We can just have a wash tomorrow…!" answered Emma.

Mom and Dad smiled to themselves and followed the children up the stairs, to prepare them for a bath and then bed.

Later that evening, Mom and Dad were finally relaxing next to one another on the couch, each drinking a small glass of wine and watching one of the many holiday movies on the television. Dad stared over at the Christmas tree for a moment. "You know what, love?"

"What's that?"

"I really do think it's the best Christmas tree we've ever had. Just look at it!"

She laughed and softly patted his chest. "Yes, it's lovely, just like you..." she said, and kissed him. "Come on, let's get to bed. I'm exhausted." She got up from the couch and grabbed his hand to help him up.

"Ugh!" groaned Dad, stretching his back. "I think I've hurt my back from dragging in that tree." He hobbled over to turn off the tree lights.

"Really? Are you going to be okay?" asked Mom, switching off the television then quietly opened the hallway door.

"Yeah, I'll be fine. I just niggled it, that's all," he sighed, and finished unplugging the tree lights from the wall. The room dropped into darkness.

Dad carefully placed the guard over the fireplace, its glowing embers lighting his way to the hallway door. He took a last glance out of the window to see the large white snowflakes falling gently into the garden. He stretched his back again and with a yawn, slowly closed the hallway door behind them both.

They made their way quietly up the stairs to bed, to what was going to be a peaceful night's sleep, for them at least.

III

The Wakeup

HE QUIET OF THE HOUSE settled around the living room, and only the occasional creak from the cooling floorboards gave any sense of life. The family had fallen fast asleep, and the grandfather clock in the hallway chimed one o'clock. Only a sliver of light from the streetlamp outside cut through the living room and shimmered across the middle of the tree.

The tree rested quietly in its new home in the corner of the room, as the odd crackle from the dying embers of the fireplace occasionally broke the peaceful silence.

Suddenly a movement rustled a branch and stopped abruptly. It was a shiny string of silver tinsel, slithering from branch to branch. A small piece, mind you, but definitely tinsel. It seemed to sniff as it passed each ornament, smelling them, looking for something.

Then there was another movement, this time from a different area of the tree, then another and another. Suddenly, and as if by magic, the whole tree was coming to life. This was the secret world of the festive Tree-Dwellers. All the character ornaments hung up on the family tree had magically awakened from a year of slumber.

All the ornaments that had arms and legs, and rotating parts, were now moving them. They yawned and stretched their bodies as they familiarized themselves with this year's Christmas tree. The sound of voices and laughter filled the branches, while the silver tinsel continued on its way.

Some of the tree lights sprang out of their sockets and lit up, their bright white light bringing the tree to life. The ornaments slipped off their branches, and began wandering around the tree to re-unite themselves with one another. Part of the greeting ritual was to offer each other freshly pulled pine needles off the tree to suck on after such a long sleep.

Cheers of joy and happy voices resounded all around the tree. "Hey, Clarence! Did you hear Mrs. Ferguson just before?" croaked a deep voice from amongst the branches. "Santa Claus apparently knows us *personally*, she said. *Ha!* If only…!"

"Yeah! As if he has the time for a chat when he's leaving the presents each year…" laughed another. "I almost felt like opening my eyes and telling her…! Be nice though…! Eh!"

The piece of Tinsel sniffing around the fresh branches of the tree stopped underneath a particular set of dangling feet. He began shaking and vibrating his body excitedly and making a strange shimmering noise. He wagged his tail and jumped up at the feet, trying to lick them, although it was difficult to tell where his tongue actually was amongst the strands of sparkling silver.

All of a sudden the dangling feet started to wiggle and a kind gentle voice laughed, "Hey, Tinsel, hey boy… Ooh, stop it, you're tickling me!" It was Larry, Tinsel's master, a large white snowman hanging from an extra large branch. He wore a long creamy white sweater with snowflake patterns that hung down past his knees. Four black buttons marched down the front of his tummy and the big brown hat on his head tastefully matched the red and white scarf and his red gloves. Over his shoulder, he held a small Christmas tree, shaped just like an umbrella, which he always had with him wherever he went.

Larry stretched and yawned. "Are you okay, boy…? Wow! Now that *was* a good sleep." He looked up and swung the umbrella handle over the branch above him, then lifted his weight off the string that was holding him up from the top of his hat. Nudging his weight closer and closer to the end of the branch, he made it bend and smoothly slipped off onto the branch below. Tinsel frantically jumped up and smothered Larry with affection, his back end wagging with uncontrollable excitement.

They were both overjoyed to see one another. Larry knelt down and hugged Tinsel, as Tinsel licked and climbed all over him.

"Come on boy, let's go and find everyone," laughed Larry. He stood up and they began making their way around the tree to look for family and friends, eager to see where everyone had been put on the tree this year.

"*Hi, Larry!*" called a voice from the branches.

Larry stopped and looked around to see where it was coming from.

"Hey! *Up here!*"

"Oh! Hi, Darrel...!" smiled Larry, waving up to him. "How are you doing?"

Darrel was a very tall and slim-looking snowman, made up of five snowballs stacked on top of one another. A big black hat sat lopsided on his head and two green holly leaves with red berries hung fashionably around his neck, resembling a bow-tie. He did not have any legs under all the snowballs, but did have a flat oval disk that he hopped around on very happily.

"I'm good, thanks Larry," nodded Darrel.

"And did you sleep well?" Larry asked fondly.

"Oh like a flippin' log, Larry! Just wonderfully!" replied Darrel, with a beaming smile. "Oh and look where they put me this year!" He opened his arms in proud satisfaction, inviting a look around.

Larry looked out and away to admire Darrel's view. "Wow!" nodded Larry. It was truly an impressive view of the living room from this point on the tree. "It's a far cry from last year, being stuck near the back of the tree."

Darrel pointed excitedly at Larry. "You have a wonderful time this season, my dear friend," and glanced at Tinsel. "You too, Tinsel. I'm going to find Sydney. She's going to be blown away by my new 'real estate'!"

Larry chuckled. He was happy that Darrel had found himself in such a good spot this year. "You do that Darrel, and Terrence and I will join you for the traditional 'Pine-Party' at your place a little later, after I've caught up with Debbie. That is, of course, if it's on again this year?"

"You bet it is! And make sure you bring that lovely lady of yours, too," winked Darrel with a grin. "You know what Sydney 'n her are like when they get going... Two peas in a flippin' pod they are... I'll catch you in a bit!"

"Sure thing!" waved Larry, and Darrel hurried quickly off behind the thick pine branches.

Larry continued with Tinsel around the tree, bumping into old friends who were still getting back into the swing of things after the big sleep.

All of a sudden, while not looking where he was going, Larry bumped into someone, who yelled with surprise and fell dramatically down onto the branch with a small *'thump'*. The fall seemed a little overacted, like someone on stage at a theater.

Larry peered down to notice a woman-like character who had cute little antlers poking out of her head. She was a cross between a young woman and a reindeer; with large appealing eyes, a small button nose, a fluffy tail, and two long legs all the way down to her small hoof-like feet.

Tinsel ran over to smother her with excitement.

"Oh! So sorry, madam…!" bumbled Larry, putting on a rather pompous voice. "Are you okay? It was *completely* my fault. I need to look where I'm *jolly* well going!" Larry gently helped her to her feet as Tinsel continued jumping at her. "Tinsel, stop it, that's rude!" continued Larry. "Are you still in one piece, madam?"

"Why, yes, I'm… I'm fine, thank you… *sir*," replied the reindeer woman, brushing herself off.

Larry harrumphed a few times, trying to impress upon her that he was a man of distinction, strong and debonair… at least for a tree ornament. Tinsel was still climbing all over the unfortunate woman. "Tinsel, stop it…! I'm so sorry about this," apologized Larry, "but there's just no stopping the boy when he gets this excited." Larry casually flicked his umbrella up onto his shoulder. "When he sees something he likes, there's no stopping him…! A chip off the old block, one would say."

"Well, that does seem to be the case, sir!" came the reply. The woman was seemingly unruffled by his self-assuredness. "Pardon me, but it's often been said around these 'ere-parts sir, that they *do* tend to take after their master." With that, she curtseyed slightly.

"Oh… I… wouldn't know about that…" answered Larry, with an air of dismissal, and casually swung his umbrella down in front of him. "So, young lady…" he said, leaning in on the umbrella to get a closer look at the young woman. "What may they call you around these 'ere-parts?"

The umbrella suddenly slipped from the branch, shaking Larry.

"It's Debbie, sir," she replied, trying her best not to laugh at his clumsiness.

"That's a *very* nice name you have there," stuttered Larry, regaining his footing. He paused for a moment, then cleared his throat and began looking a little awkward with what he was about to ask. "Well, Debbie. Would you mind… Em. Well, with it being Christmas and all, I was wondering if you'd like to…"

Suddenly, Debbie kissed him on the cheek, taking him by surprise.

Larry's body began swaying and his eyes glazed over. "Um… are we there yet?" he stuttered as one of the black buttons on his sweater popped off and fell onto the branch below.

They both laughed at one another and lovingly embraced, completely overwhelmed by being back together again after so many months.

"Hi, Debbie."

"Hi, Larry," she replied, looking up at his smiling face, while fiddling with one of his buttons. "Did you sleep okay?"

"Oh yeah," sighed Larry. "What a sleep…! Wow…! And how about you?"

"Wonderfully..." she smiled. "But I missed you."

"Me too…" smiled Larry, stroking her hair with his large red glove.

They pulled away slowly and smiled in admiration at one another.

"So I'm going to grab my brother," explained Larry, "and I'll catch up with you shortly, okay?"

"Sure... and give him a big kiss for me, won't you!"

"Eeew…!" Larry joked, as though kissing his own brother was an awful thought. "Oh, and by the way," he remembered, "Darrel's invited us all up for 'Pine-Snacking' a little later."

"You mean you invited yourself up there again!" replied Debbie, with a knowing look on her face.

Larry held his stomach. "Well yeah, you know, he somehow always seems to get the freshest pines from around the tree. After all this time, I still don't know how he does it… Anyway, you're on for it, yeah…?"

"Sure! I'll see you shortly," nodded Debbie.

Larry looked down at Tinsel, who was staring at Debbie as she walked away. "Hey! Come on boy, let's go," he called, tapping his side.

"*Oh Larrrryyyy...!*" called a soft voice from behind him. He turned his head to see Debbie blow a kiss. Larry followed the invisible kiss with his eyes, as though on fluttering wings, all the way over to him, and *'wallop!'* It smacked him on the lips. His head re-coiled and he blinked with amazement at its punch. Larry smiled, and without a sound escaping from his lips whispered, "Love you."

Debbie turned away wagging her little tail, satisfied, and admittedly slightly giddy, too.

Larry glanced back at Tinsel, who was staring at him. "*What?*" shrugged Larry. "Come on. Let's find that flippin' brother of mine..." and continued on their way through the branches.

"*Hi, Jerry!*" called Larry, waving to a small Christmas lantern a couple of branches away. It had its front door open and the candle inside was pulling off a pine needle from a very sweet and tender looking branch.

"I said... *Hi, Jerry!*" repeated Larry a little louder. Jerry stopped picking and opened up one of his side doors as though he was listening intently.

"Down here, pal!" smiled Larry, and waved both his arms around to get his attention.

"Oh... Hi, Larry!" laughed Jerry, finally noticing the waving arms. "I didn't know where that voice was coming from," he said, chuckling. "I'm sure I'm getting more wax in my ears every year, you know. I can't hear a thing these days."

"Not a chance, Jerry! I think every year my voice just gets a little quieter," laughed Larry, steadying himself on the branch with his tree-umbrella. "So, I was wondering, Jerry! I don't suppose you've seen Terrence around yet, have you...?"

Jerry shook his head. "No... Not me... I've only just woken up myself..." and yawned aloud. "Oh, *excuse me*...! Where the-diddly did that come from?" he smiled. "Ooh...! I can't believe how comfy that little box of mine was this last time. Hope I get it again, it was lovely."

"Here's hoping for you, Jerry," nodded Larry. "Well, if you do happen to see Terrence, tell him I'm looking for him."

"Will do!" replied Jerry, and he glanced up at a branch just above him. "I've just found some really juicy pine-treats for the Carnival. They're oh so soft right around here you know."

"Thanks for the heads up, Jerry!" nodded Larry. "I'll see you later," and he continued on his way, with Tinsel by his side.

Joy and festivities were going on all around the tree. The lights, which the dwellers fondly called the 'Army-Lights', marched up and down the tree, replacing each other's shifts at the bottom. They had the important job of keeping all the dwellers safe and sound from the unknown dangers that lurked out there away from the tree.

Larry continued to pass friends and neighbors from previous years. He stopped to talk and reminisce about the years before, and what joys this festive time would bring. However, considering they had now been awake for some time, Larry assumed he would have seen his brother by now, or at least know of his whereabouts. No one else seemed to have seen him yet either, and although it was great to see everyone back on the tree again this year, he needed to find Terrence before joining in on the festivities.

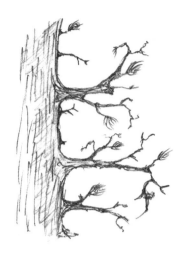

IV

Away From The Carnival

FTER WANDERING AROUND THE TREE a while longer, Larry realized that both he and Tinsel had covered a large area of the front, and were now quite high up. Now the easiest path from branch to branch was about to take them around towards the back of the tree. Larry took a last look at the festivities going on around and below him, and a short-lived smile dropped off his face. He turned and walked into the darker and quieter area of the tree, where most dwellers had little or no need to venture.

The view of an ever-darkening wall now replaced the inviting living room, as Larry and Tinsel stepped ever deeper into the darkness. Larry noticed the thick lush branches from the front of the tree were replaced by ever thinning ones, almost completely starved of pine needles. Larry felt his heart drop, as this was definitely not an area of the tree he would like to find himself waking up in.

He continued on and noticed how much weaker the branches were at the back of the tree; some were beginning to flex and crack under his weight. In addition to this, the sheer lack of needles on the branches were making it increasingly slippery and dangerous under foot.

Meanwhile, Tinsel, being light and flexible, took it all in his stride, and repeatedly ran ahead, only to stop and wait for his struggling master to catch up.

Larry stepped tentatively, regularly hooking the handle of his trusted umbrella onto higher branches, to support his stride across the ever-widening gaps. He knew all too well that this was a very dangerous area of the tree for him. Being made of glass, even a small fall through the branches could break him. He was admittedly not the most agile of Tree-Dwellers, and would never leave his Bedtime-Branch without his trusted umbrella, which regularly helped him get around the awkward bits of the tree.

Larry stopped for a moment. *"Terrence...!"* he called, *"Terrence...!"* then listened intently, hoping for a reply.

There was nothing; only a deafening silence echoed around the branches. Not even the noise from the festivities he left at the front of the tree could be heard this far inside the back. The level of darkness he found himself in was only matched by the quietness, as an unsettling feeling suddenly scurried up his spine.

He sighed and turned to Tinsel. "He's not here is he b—" His words were interrupted by a mighty 'CRACK', and he felt himself falling. *"NOOOO!"* Larry instinctively reached out with the handle of his umbrella, which luckily caught a branch and stopped his fall. Tinsel barked and tried running over to him.

"Uh…! No, boy…!" warned Larry. "Stay!" and frantically looked around to assess the situation. He took an uneasy glance down below him to see a couple of thin branches, before a huge drop to the presents at the very bottom of the tree.

He knew he had just been incredibly lucky and glanced anxiously at Tinsel. "Ugh…! Now that could have been a bit nasty, hey, boy…!" He swallowed hard and carefully climbed back up.

Larry took a moment to compose himself before trying to find his bearings. "So, where do you think we are Tinsel boy…? I think we might have actually got ourselves lost here!" laughing nervously to himself. He brushed his hand across a skinny branch with only a couple of brown needles clinging to it. "Well there's not much food here, wherever we are," then squinted through the bleak darkness. "Okay! Terrence isn't here, or I'm sure we'd have seen him by now. I bet he's looking for us both around the front of the tree! That'd be typical of him! Hey, boy…?" Tinsel wagged his tail. "Come on then! Let's get out of here… If we keep on walking around in the same direction, we'll sooner or later get back to the front."

From now on, Larry chose his branches more carefully, making doubly sure they were strong enough to hold him. Finally he noticed that everything was getting brighter and the branches were becoming thicker with healthier and tastier looking pine needles.

He quickened his pace, thinking of how long he had been at the back of the tree. He hoped his idea was right, and his brother was now looking for him at the front. After all, he had been searching the back of the tree for a while, giving Terrence more than enough time to wake up from his Bedtime-Branch, wherever that was.

As the darkness of the tree fell back behind him, Larry felt even more upbeat and excited about getting back to the front, convinced he'd just been too eager and impatient to find Terrence.

All of a sudden from above, a little closed pinecone fell down in front of Larry, making him jump. "Whoa there young fellow…!" laughed Larry, placing out his hands to steady it.

"Hi, Little-Cone," said Larry, gently tapping the top of the cone. Larry watched as the outer pieces of the pinecone slowly opened from the top like a hedgehog, and a little head popped out.

"Oh… Sorry, Mister Larry! I didn't see you there…!" gasped the pinecone, giggling up at Larry. "I just did a 'Triple-Pine Swing'… *A triple!* Did you see it, Mister Larry?"

Before Larry could answer, Little-Cone yelled excitedly up into the branches, "*Did you see it? And I didn't fall either!*"

"*Nah…!* Doesn't count. Mister Larry stopped you from

falling," answered his twin brother 'Little-Pine' from several branches above.

The 'Spin-a-Branch' game involved spinning around a chosen pine branch by their hands as fast as possible, then jumping off and landing on a chosen branch lower down, without falling over from the dizziness.

"Ah! A *'Triple-Pine Swing'* … Three times eh…! Wow, *that's great!*" exclaimed Larry, still smiling at Little-Cone. "So, how long had you been practicing before you managed to do three?"

"Oh, only about five seasons," bragged Little-Cone. "But just when I get good, we have to go back to sleep again for ages and ages. It's just not fair!" He began picking some sticky pine sap off one of his fingers.

"We all have to sleep."

Little-Cone ignored Larry's comment. "So how many spins can you do, Mister Larry?"

Larry chuckled and held out his arm. "Tap this. Go on...!" Little-Cone inquisitively tapped it with his hand.

"I'm glass, you see," explained Larry. "You're made of wood. I'm not cut out for spinning around branches like you. You 'Wood Folk' are a lot more flexible and not as brittle as us 'Glass Folk'." Larry smiled. "My brother did try a 'Single-Swing' a while ago… but he fell off the branch, so I guess that didn't count."

"Yeah! That doesn't count! And my brother… My brother up there can do *two* 'Triple-Pine Swings'. One after the other!"

"Wow...! That's impressive. Where is he?"

"My brother…? He's up there," answered Little-Cone, looking up into the branches above them. "Hey, bro! Go on! Your turn now!" Larry looked up and noticed his brother, Little-Pine, already hanging off a thick branch, ready to start his swing.

Suddenly a voice from a few branches away interrupted his preparation. "*Hey...!* I thought it was you two! Now what did I tell you about Pine-Swinging this high up in the tree?" It was Little-Pine and Little-Cone's mother, who had heard them both shouting and giggling. Neither Larry nor the twins could see her through the branches, but they could tell she wasn't happy with them both. "If I've told you both once, I've told you a thousand times...!" she continued. "You're only made of wood, you know... You hear me?"

"Oh dear!" whispered Larry. "Now you're in trouble."

"Yes, Mom..." replied the twins, as Little-Pine dropped down off his branch to join his brother, both looking really embarrassed and sheepish for being told off in front of Larry.

"This is your last warning, the pair of you!" continued their mother with pointed fingers. "Now get down to the lower branches where I told you to play, where it's not far to fall. Beautiful as you both are, you won't look too pretty broken into little pieces by the time Santa arrives, will you...?"

"No, Mom," sighed the twin pinecones.

"*No-Shmoe...!* Now get down there before I tell Tree-Lord, and he has your guts for garters! Oh and make sure you keep away from that Mr. Flemming, too! I don't want him back up here again complaining like last year," and tutted, "Calling you both the 'Terror Twins'. It was so embarrassing...! Now hop-it the pair o' you!"

Larry tried not to smile, watching the two pinecones scurry past him down towards the lower branches, blaming one another for getting found out. "I told you! I knew she'd hear us as soon as you started counting…!" accused Little-Cone.

"No way…!" defended his brother. "It was *your* flippin' fault for yelling out *'I'm going for four…! Going for four!'*" They both giggled, pushing one another down off the branches.

"I could have done a fourth you know, if I wanted to," bragged Little-Cone. "But that triple was good, eh? You see it…? Weeeeeeeee…! And did you see how high I was too? I bet no one's *ever* done one that high before! *No one!*"

"Yeah, whatever!" sighed Little-Pine, sounding unconvinced, and they finally disappeared out of sight below the lower branches.

Larry and Tinsel had just started continuing on their way, when Larry heard his name being called through the branches and immediately recognized the voice, "Debbie…! Is that you?"

"*Yes…! Where are you?*" she replied, sounding excited and out of breath.

Larry's face lit up. "She's found my brother… Come on boy!" and they quickly made their way towards her voice.

"*I'm here… I'm here, Debbie!*" called Larry, making his way frantically from branch to branch. Debbie appeared, completely out of breath and Larry grabbed her with open arms.

"Where have you been, Larry?"

"I just went around the back of the tree to look for Terrence…!" he said, glancing over her shoulder. "Where is he?"

Debbie's face dropped and she gently shook her head, knowing what he must have thought.

"You still haven't found him?"

"No, Larry! And I was worried about you. I didn't know where you'd gone either… You've been away for ages."

Larry pulled away. "No… no… no!" His heart dropped like a stone. "I don't believe this! Where could he have gotten to?"

Debbie did not know what to say and twiddled her fingers nervously, wishing she had better news for him. "Look! We still have a lot of time left before morning sleep. We'll keep on looking until we find him… Okay?"

Larry nodded and they made their way anxiously back around the tree, where everyone was happily going about their business. Debbie was determined not to let Larry out of her sight from now on, and they both began calling for Terrence through the hustle and bustle at the front of the tree.

V

Finding A Name

LARRY'S LOUD VOICE HAD CARRIED ITSELF OVER to a different area on the tree, and had helped finally wake up the new wooden ornament the children were given earlier in the evening. He was hanging there, his body painted red; which gave the impression he wore a red jacket. He had a white painted stripe all the way down his front to the shiny black belt around his waist, and had distinctive gold paint on both shoulders. His white glove-like hands went well with his red trousers and shiny black boots, and on his head he wore a red hat that was attached to the thick pine branch.

A couple of neighborly Tree-Dwellers; a brown Christmas rabbit and a wind-up-toy made of metal, had been patiently sucking on some pine needles, waiting for the new dweller to wake up.

Finally the new dweller yawned loudly and slowly opened his

eyes.

The two dwellers quickly made their way over to introduce themselves, eager to welcome him to the tree.

The rabbit smiled and nodded at him. His big floppy ears, bright green scarf and tartan cap seemed a contradiction to his small round eyeglasses.

The two dwellers briefly gazed up at him, then without asking, grabbed his arms and lifted him down off the branch.

With a smile, the wind-up-toy offered up a freshly plucked pine needle from the tree. "Here you go my good fellow. Get some sustenance into you after that long sleep."

The soldier stared at them both, before taking the pine needle and copied what they were doing by slowly sucking on it. He still looked a little confused as to where he was, and was obviously overwhelmed by such a friendly reception.

"So, what did they call you then…?" asked the rabbit, chuckling a little.

There was a short but awkward pause, as the new character looked blankly back at them both.

"Well, I'm Max," announced the rabbit, twitching his nose and correcting his glasses. "And this good friend of mine over here is Dan."

Dan nodded with a smile.

There was another long pause, while the new character gazed around the tree and out into the living room, still wondering where he'd found himself.

"Were you not given a name by the family?" asked Max inquisitively. "Not even the kids?" and waited a moment before rubbing his hands together excitedly. "Wow, this *is* a pleasure indeed then! If they didn't give you one," continued Max, correcting the cap on his head, "It's tradition around here that we have the honor of finding one for you. Isn't that so, Dan?"

"That it is, Max."

"What?" asked the new dweller, looking rather bewildered.

"Everyone who arrives on the tree," continued Max, "is either given a name by the family, or the task is betrothed upon the first Tree-Dwellers who introduce themselves. So that's me and me good mate Dan," Max turned to Dan. "So what do you think…?"

Dan was intently sucking on a pine needle, looking the new dweller up and down, deep in concentration.

The new character was still totally bewildered and struggling to catch up with his new environment and a buzz of activity he had never encountered before.

Dan began the proceedings. "So! Let's see now! What are you made of, my good man?"

"Hardwood… Um, wood I think," came the hesitant reply.

"*I got it…!* How 'bout *'Plank'?*" smiled Dan, looking proud of himself.

Max looked confusingly round at him. "*You're kidding me! 'Plank!'* You really think that anyone in their right mind would want to be called… *'Plank'?*"

Dan shrugged his shoulders.

"No… No…!" dismissed Max, and turned back to the new dweller. "So, you're wood, eh… Do you happen to know where you originally came from?"

"No, not exactly," replied the new dweller, shaking his head a little. "A basket! A basket in a shop."

Dan and Max laughed a little. They were hoping more for an area of the world, or maybe a big city. "Ooh, we are in a pickle now, aren't we!" pondered Max, twitching his nose a little then turned away thinking.

The new dweller glanced at Dan, and noticed he had stopped moving and was standing completely still, staring blankly back at him. "Um... Max," called the new dweller with concern.

But Max was thinking too hard to hear anyone and was mumbling to himself. "Okay then! So he's made of wood. *That* we surely know. So, um..." He suddenly jumped excitedly back around. "'Splint'! How 'bout 'Splint', like wood! Yeah, how 'bout that then? That fits, hey!?"

"Excuse me Max," repeated the new dweller. "I think something's happened to your friend here," and pointed at Dan, standing motionless.

"Oh...!" sighed Max, looking unconcerned. "Not to worry, it's all good." He walked briskly over and around the back of Dan, and gently wound up a key that was slotted into his back. After a few turns, Max walked back around and shouted in Dan's face, "*You back with us there mate...?*"

Dan began moving, slowly at first, then finally back up to full speed. "*Yeah, 'Splinter!' Great one...!*"

"*No,*" sighed Max. "*'Splint'!*"

"Yeah, yeah...! That's what I said, in' it. 'Splint'... Yeah! Good one! Suits him down to a tee. So what do you say?" asked Dan, both looking eagerly back at the wooden dweller.

There was a long pause. "So...?" beckoned Dan again.

The new ornament did not know if it was a good name or not,

but not wanting to appear rude or unappreciative, he shrugged his shoulders and casually accepted. "Yeah, okay then. Yeah... Call me Splint!"

"Great stuff!" smiled Max, rubbing his hands together in proud satisfaction. "Let's give you the tour." They began to lead Splint slowly away across the branches. "Now that your name's settled, Splint, let us be so kind as to show you around this place, so you feel more at home.... Oh, and before we forget! You need to remember which branch you woke up from," and pointed back at the branch. "That's what you call your Bedtime-Branch. You'll need to be back up there when the lights start coming up from the tree floor..."

Dan added, "We don't want anything outside the tree to know about us eh...?" and winked with a nod and a smile.

"Yeah... I mean no...!" replied Splint, who was still a little unsure of these two characters, his new name and the world he now found himself in.

At the other side of the tree, Larry and Debbie were now feeling as though they had all but exhausted their search for Terrence. They had looked everywhere they could possibly think of. Debbie knew that by now, someone somewhere should have seen him on their travels, but she kept her concern to herself for fear of Larry losing all hope.

Larry walked past Harold and Margaret, two wooden Christmas trees that had been meticulously carved out of the same piece of wood many years ago by the family's Great Grandad. Harold was walking, as always, just slightly in front of Margaret, and they were hastily on their way to find a good branch from which to view the upcoming 'Wakeup Carnival'.

"Excuse me," said Larry, struggling to hold back his frustration. "We're still looking for Terrence. I don't suppose either of you have seen him around, have you?"

"No, I'm sorry Larry," shrugged Harold, who although a slightly thicker and taller tree than Margaret, did not have Margaret's shiny golden stripes on his body, or the star that stuck out on the top of her head. "We haven't, have we Margaret. Debbie asked us both earlier on…" and nodded over Larry's shoulder to acknowledge Debbie.

Larry sighed and dropped his head. He began to feel now as though he would never find his brother. There was an awkward moment as Margaret and Harold briefly glanced at one another.

"Look, Larry… We're sorry," said Margaret. "You know we care about you, don't you?" she said, placing a hand gently on his shoulder. "We understand it's difficult… But might it be easier to accept that he simply didn't make it back this year, and move on?"

Larry's heart finally sank after hearing the same thing from Margaret, as he had been hearing from other dwellers. This made him feel they must all be right. After all the hopeless searching, he had to accept that for whatever the reason, he would not see his brother ever again.

Harold nodded with understanding. "It just happens lad… So chin up." He turned to Margaret. "We'd better go find those branches before they're gone," and gave a quick glance over to Debbie, before walking away.

Debbie stepped up slowly behind Larry, wrapped her arms

around his big chest, and squeezed him gently. She was desperately wondering what she could say or do to make him feel better. "Why don't we ask Tree-Lord? I know he doesn't like being disturbed, but this is really important to you. He might know something."

Larry shook his head. "No… I don't want to bother him. He'll just say the same as everyone else; *'He didn't make it back. So just move on!'*" and glanced over to the ever-increasing dwellers gathering for the 'Wakeup Carnival'. "They all think I'm overreacting. They all do…" Larry shook his head. "Doesn't anyone remember him?"

"They do Larry, but they just think differently about it," answered Debbie with a heavy sigh. She could tell from his shallow breathing that he was crying, and squeezed him affectionately, gently resting the side of her head on his back.

He took a deep breath and removed her hands from around him and quickly wiped the tears from his face. Debbie felt useless, not knowing what to do to help Larry through his grief.

In another area of the tree, Splint, Max and Dan were continuing their tour around the branches. Dan was explaining to Splint what the best tasting needles looked like, and how the flavors differed depending on what area of the tree the needles were picked from. "You see Splint, up near the top is where you'll find the freshest, lightest tasting needles. They're a bit too… um... light tasting for me. We much prefer the ones at the very tips of these here middle branches, don't we Max…!" He picked one, looked at it, then passed it to Splint to taste. Dan continued, "You'll find them slightly more complex in flavor than the ones at the top, you know…" Dan nodded intently while watching Splint bite into it. "But not as bitter as those-there ones on the lower branches see… Ugh… Terrible down there, bitter as you like," and paused for a moment, causing Splint to think he needed winding up again. Suddenly Dan piped up again. "But some like that bitterness. It's all up to the individual. Isn't that so Max?"

Max nodded eagerly.

Splint's attention was drawn away to the branches where Larry had earlier been shouting for his brother. "What's the matter with the snowman over there? What was he shouting about?" he asked inquisitively, still sucking on the needle.

"Who…Oh Larry?" answered Max. "Oh… I think he was still looking for that brother of his, Terrence. Not sure if he made it to the tree this year, me thinks… Hey, Dan?"

Splint was confused by the comment. "Didn't make it! What do you mean…? Why didn't he make it to the tree?" and glanced back out at Larry.

"Well you see, Splint," began Dan, finding a comfortable branch to sit on, as though he was settling into a long story, "That's what happens here. Here on the tree… Sometimes you don't make it back the following year… That's the way it's always been."

"Really?" asked Splint, looking concerned. "*Always been! Why's that?*"

"Why...? Don't know, do we Max," shrugged Dan, suddenly wondering why he had never thought of asking it himself.

"Tree-Lord! Maybe you should go an' ask him," suggested Max. "He might have the answer for ya!"

"Tree-Lord! Who's that?"

"He's our Tree Elder," explained Dan. "The loving and wise protector of our tree society."

"And where's he?"

"As always, there's only one place you'll find him, and that's near the top, up there…" pointed Max, and he continued with a quieter voice. "He's up there, stuck in the wire of the lighting… You'll never see him down here… Oh, no, no, no sir… He doesn't move you see… He just stays up there… looking out for us all and taking care of the community… That's what he does ya see, for the whole of this here twelve days of Christmas."

Suddenly there was commotion coming from all the dwellers around the tree. "Ooh, the 'Wakeup Carnival' is about to start," clapped Dan, acting overly excited. "Come on! Come on!" and beckoned them both to climb with him to a better branch for viewing the extravaganza.

A deep loud voice echoed above everyone's heads. Everyone stopped talking and gazed up towards the top of the tree.

It was Tree-Lord, ready to begin the 'Wakeup Carnival'.

Tree-Lord was a large orange light in the shape of a tree-cone, with two arms at each side of his body and a small face shaped into his front. For reasons unknown to anyone on the tree, he had been screwed and riveted tightly into his socket at the top of the lighting cable, rendering him immobile. The up side of this was that Tree-Lord could communicate with the Army-Lights by flashing to them, and the Lights would happily attend to his every need, helping him to protect the Tree-Dwellers from the outside world.

Tree-Lord began the Wakeup Carnival as he did every year, by addressing the dwellers as one big family and leading them all in a wonderful festive song, which welcomed everyone to the tree again, especially the new arrivals.

In the song, he would remind everyone the way of living in harmony on the tree is to obey the laws that define their society, and how important it was for everyone to be back on their Bedtime-Branches before daylight. Tree-Lord continued by explaining the boundary of lights at the bottom of the tree, made up of 'Army-Lights' that protect the dwellers from the dangers outside, warning them never to venture further than the lighting permits.

The song increased in intensity and everyone sang and danced up and down along the branches. The lights were jumping up and out of their sockets into the air, perfectly synchronized, and as their paths crossed they deliberately touched one another's wires, causing sparks to cascade like fireworks down onto the parade. Everyone cheered at the sparkling display and continued in the celebrations.

Everyone, that is, except Larry.

VI

From Somewhere

HE SONG FINALLY ENDED, and the tree continued to bustle with excitement and happiness, as everyone looked forward to the rest of the upcoming festivities.

After clapping and hooting with wild joy, Dan and Max settled down on two thick branches to continue chewing on their pine needles. Splint just stood there, still trying to take everything in that was going on around him. Although impressed with the carnival celebrations, Splint continued to wonder about Larry and glanced back over to him and Debbie. He noticed Debbie's shoulders drop in reaction to Larry's words, then Larry turned and walked away with a sadness in his step. They both looked out of sorts in contrast to everyone else on the tree. He watched Debbie gesture to Tinsel to follow his master – to give him company and keep him safe. Debbie awkwardly glanced across the tree and noticed Splint's stare, then quickly turned away.

Splint's attention was suddenly drawn to a dweller passing by on a branch below. It was not her crooked nose or the green complexion, or in fact the pointed hat, broomstick or striped stockings that caught his attention; it was her mumbling and really bad temper.

"Where *is* that sister of mine…?" she grunted, and pushed a small house to the side that was hanging in her way, sending it swinging wildly backwards and forwards. Splint continued to watch the curious woman as she dropped down onto a lower branch, still mumbling and huffing to herself. She turned around and began walking the other way, under the swinging house, when suddenly the house slipped from its branch and fell. Splint tried warning her, but it was too late, *'Bang!'*

"*Ooh…!*" cried the woman below. Splint cringed in sympathy at how that must have hurt and glanced back to Dan and Max, who were both chuckling to one another about something completely different; they had not seen the woman at all. "Hey! She's…!" began Splint, not making any sense at all. They looked up and then down to where he was pointing.

"Oh, her!" dismissed Max, realizing what Splint was talking about. "She's fine, don't worry. That house falls on her *every year*, without fail!" and leaned forward whispering, "For attention we think," and held out a pine needle. "Now come and join us for a small 'Pine-Party'.

"That darn house…!" the old woman mumbled. "I'll get that Dorothy if it's the last thing I do!"

Splint grinned. Even though she was overly grumpy, he found her quite endearing, and watched her limp away out of sight under the branches.

He turned back to join Dan and Max for that snack, when a loud voice startled him. "All right there, me-ole cock-sparrow?" Splint turned to see a Chimney Sweeper greeting him with a big smile. The man was holding a large brush in one hand and had black soot painted all over his clothes and face.

"Sorry…?" replied Splint, struggling with the character's odd accent. "What…? What did you say…?"

Max and Dan, lying down on the branches, chuckled to one another. "Hi there, Van-Deek," called Max. "How's it going…?" and raised an arm in the air. "It's going to be a good one this year, we thinks…!" and nodded back over to Van-Deek.

Van-Deek smiled over at them both. "All right there, chaps…?" he inquired, tipping his hat in acknowledgment, then turned to Splint, who was still looking a little startled.

"Oh, where are our manners," Max said standing up, still sucking a pine needle in the side of his mouth. "Van-Deek… Let us introduce 'Splint'. He's new to the tree this year, would you believe!"

"That I would!" nodded Van-Deek, in an upbeat Cockney-London accent. He spat into his right hand and wiped it on his leg, before holding it out to Splint. "Yes, Van-Deek's the name… How do ya do!"

Unsure of what Van-Deek was asking, Splint held out his hand in a similar manner and asked, "How do I do what…?" He hoped Van-Deek would repeat the question with a little more clarity.

Van-Deek grabbed Splint's hand and pumped it firmly, and affectionately slapped him on the shoulder, laughing along with Dan and Max to Splint's question. "Splint! Welcome to the tree, young fellow. I truly hope your seasons here will be as joyous and fruitful for you as they have been all these years for our good selves." He glanced to Dan and Max and nodded. "Anyway, it's been a pleasure gentlemen, but I must be off…" and touched his dusty hat, bowed, and bid them all a fond farewell.

Splint looked down at his black sooty hand, still puzzled and somewhat frustrated at not understanding what Van-Deek had asked. Wiping the hand on his leg, he glanced over to where Debbie and Larry had been talking earlier, and noticed Debbie walking solemnly away, occasionally looking down towards the bottom of the tree. He followed her glances and caught Larry jumping down off the last branch to disappear into the small pile of presents under the tree.

Splint was making his way back towards Dan and Max when a brightly lit Army-Light jumped down off a branch above him, catching him off guard.

Splint thought for a moment, then placed a hand out to the light. "My name's Splint. How do ya do?" he said, trying his best to copy Van-Deek's accent. But to his surprise, the light ignored him. It hopped down onto a lower branch and sped away.

Max and Dan immediately burst into laughter and rolled around on the branches, making Splint feel even more frustrated and confused.

"Oh, sorry Splint," apologized Max, seeing the frustration on Splint's face. "You see, the lights can't communicate with us. Tree-Lord's the only one who can understand their strange 'WOO-HOO' flashing language," then paused momentarily. "And somehow he can talk back to them, too."

"So look, Splint," said Dan, still composing himself after laughing so hard. "This just might help you a bit. Everyone… I mean everyone on the tree is from somewhere special. Like your good self, somewhere outside these four walls, from far away lands like good old Van-Deek there for example. We've all arrived on the tree to signify a special occasion in this here family's life." He looked at Max. "Like my good friend here, who was added to celebrate their eighth Wedding Anniversary… And Van-Deek who you just met… came back with them from one of their trips to that there rainy place… You know… What's it called now…?" He clicked his fingers frantically, looking down and away, trying to think where it was.

Max got up off the branch and continued on from Dan. " That is *why* Splint, we've grown into a very impressive family… and that makes this tree so special… so *very* special…" He smiled while looking around the tree, before turning back to Splint. "So tell me Splint, just for the record, so to speak. What kind of *basket* were you from in the shop and do you know what the special occasion was for them bringing you to the tree?"

"Um…" replied Splint, feeling uneasy with the question. Max was about to say something more, when another Army-Light returning from its duty at the bottom of the tree accidentally knocked into him. Its light was dim and inconsistent, and it was struggling to keep its balance, wobbling from side to side.

Max watched with concern as the light went by, worried that it was going to fall off the tree. "Whoa-there, fella! *Poor guy*. He's totally exhausted." He waited for the light to get a little higher and out of sight before starting his sentence. He glanced at the pine needle in his hand and, noticing it had been sucked of all its goodness, began choosing a fresh one from a branch close by. After finally picking a needle he was happy with, he turned to reengage Splint with the question. "So, Splint. *Oh...!*" he exclaimed, surprised to see that Splint had completely disappeared. "Where's he gone...?"

"*Greenland!*" interrupted Dan, jumping to his feet. "Yeah! That's it! Greenland! I knew it was something like that!"

"What? Splint's gone to... *Greenland?*" asked Max, looking bewildered.

"Yeah! Where Van-Deek's from. He was sayin' it was really flippin' green there."

"What...? What are you talking about?"

Dan looked around the branches. "Hey! Where's Splint gone?"

Max rolled his eyes and sighed, then slapped Dan across the back of the head with his hat.

VII

How Do You Do

DOWN AT THE BOTTOM OF THE TREE, Larry nestled quietly amongst the wrapped presents, staring blankly into space. A discarded pine needle fell onto his shoulder that he barely reacted to. "Sorry... Didn't see you down there!" called a voice from the branches above. Larry nodded absently and continued his empty stare.

A rustling noise appeared by Larry's side. It was Tinsel, who sat down quietly next to Larry and nudged his nose and head under his hand, to rest on his lap. "Hey, boy..." sighed Larry, gently stroking Tinsel's head.

Larry looked out into the room and began to reflect on his brother's whereabouts, wondering if he was okay or in trouble. The unknown made Larry worry even more.

He felt totally alone; no one except for Debbie understood how he felt. Larry was usually one of the first to accept that from time to time some characters just did not make it back to the tree. Now however, he was not so sure why he was ever so accepting of that fact. Because it was now his brother who had not made it back, everything on the tree felt wrong and different. His brother would have wanted to come back to the tree, or Larry would have sensed it from him last year, before being packed away.

Tinsel's silver hair stood up on his back and he began growling, pulling Larry out of his dark place.

"Shush boy… It's okay," ordered Larry, trying to calm him down, while glancing around to see what had spooked him. A little further away he noticed two characters giggling and whispering to one another amongst the presents. They had not noticed Larry and Tinsel down there with them, and were daring one another to peek inside the wrapping paper. Larry smiled briefly, remembering back to a time when both he and Terrence would have been doing the very same thing.

"Go on, Larry… It's a sweater I tell ya… A flippin' sweater… Can't be anything else that size," Terrence said confidently.

"Go on then… Go on Mr. Confidence… I dare ya…!" answered Larry, enticing Terrence to take a peek. They giggled, and Larry noticed Terrence was off-balance while looking over the present, and pushed him for fun. Terrence fell heavily into it and they both heard the paper rip. They stopped still and

gasped at one another.

"Don't move, Terrence!" exclaimed Larry, and he carefully looked around to examine where the sound came from.

Terrence slowly lifted his right elbow. "Hey... Um... Larry," he whispered, in a concerned voice. Larry glanced over and noticed the big hole Terrence had made in the paper, just below his elbow. They stole a quick glance around to see if they had been noticed, then giggled uncontrollably, knowing the trouble they would be in if anyone found out.

Terrence carefully lifted his elbow away and with one of his thick fingers, gently pulled back the paper and they both looked inside...

Larry was pulled out of his thoughts by Tinsel, who was growling again. Larry looked up, and noticed Splint standing there in front of him.

"Hi..." said Splint. "Oh, sorry...! How do you do...!" correcting himself, as he now assumed everyone introduced themselves in the way Van-Deek had done earlier. "I'm Splint... I've just arrived on the tree from the basket, in a shop," and held out his hand.

Larry stared back for a moment, then looked behind him as though it was some kind of a joke. He shook his hand. "Hi... I'm Larry," he said, then turned away.

Splint felt awkward and was not sure how to continue the conversation, sensing Larry wanted to be left alone. He nervously cleared his drying throat. "About your brother…"

"You've seen him?" interrupted Larry, looking around anxiously.

"No… I… I just wanted to say that I'm sorry you haven't found him yet."

Larry nodded and turned back to face the ground. "Thanks…"

"Here…" said Splint, offering a soft fresh pine needle to Larry. "They're from up there around the middle. Not too bitter."

"Thanks," replied Larry, who sensed Splint's sincerity and began sucking on the pine needle.

Splint found a place to sit and looked out across the room to where Larry had been staring earlier. "So you have no idea where he could be, then…?" asked Splint gently.

Larry shook his head. "I've looked everywhere on the tree, absolutely everywhere." He sighed deeply. "I have to accept… that sometimes we don't make it back here the next year," then gazed up into the branches.

Splint stared at him for a moment, trying to read his thoughts. "So why *is* that…? Why does everyone here think that?"

"Cause that's what happens here…*Okay!*" snapped Larry, unable to contain his frustration. Listening to Splint ask the same question that had been running around in his own head ever since he woke up this year, only increased his anxiety.

Splint knew he had overstepped his mark, and nodded understandingly. Silence dropped over the conversation as they both gazed out into the dark room.

It was not long before Splint tried to reignite the

conversation. "So, he's out there somewhere then."

Larry paused a moment, digesting the comment, then looked over at Splint. "What do you mean?"

"Well you said he's not here on the tree, so he's obviously somewhere out there!"

"You think so…?" spouted Larry, taking another look out into the room. He nodded to himself, thinking of the possibility. "Yeah… Maybe he is… Maybe he's still out there!"

"Here," smiled Splint, offering Larry another pine needle, which he gladly accepted.

Larry felt a little guilty for snapping at him earlier. "I'm sorry, Splint. Where are my manners? I haven't asked anything about you. How are you finding it here on the tree? You settling in okay?"

"Well… yeah, I guess so… It's better than being alone in that basket, that's for sure."

"Basket? What basket's that…?"

Splint ignored the question and continued. "So, where was the last time you saw your brother?"

"Um…" frowned Larry, adjusting to the sudden change in conversation. He took a careful glance at Splint, and wondered why he seemed so interested in his brother's whereabouts; after all, no one else on the tree seemed to care. Larry's gut reaction was to trust him. He assumed the questioning was Splint's way of trying to settle in on the tree and make friends. "Last time...?" continued Larry. "That would be just before the box was closed last year."

"Box... What box is that?" asked Splint, shuffling his position to face Larry.

"Our Christmas box, of course," puzzled Larry, then realized Splint had yet to see it. "Oh sorry, I forgot you're new... It's the box that we're all kept safe in during the sleeping months, until this time of year comes around again."

Splint's eyes lit up and he quickly got to his feet.

"What is it, Splint...?" asked Larry.

"Hear me out for a minute," began Splint. "What's the possibility that your brother is still sleeping in that box of yours, just waiting to be brought out?" and paused a moment to gauge Larry's reaction. "Maybe they didn't see him in there. Is the box big?"

Larry's face lit up like a beacon. "*Yeah, it's really big*. It holds pretty much all of us including the lights," and smiled. "You think it's possible?"

"I don't know," shrugged Splint, backing off a little. "Why not though! I guess *anything's* possible," then chewed down hard on his pine needle.

A voice interrupted the conversation. "*Larry! Are you there...?*" It was Debbie.

"Yes. We're over here!" called Larry excitedly. She appeared from behind one of the presents.

"Hi," said Debbie, "I just wanted to make sure you—" She noticed he had company. "Oh, I'm sorry! I thought you were by yourself..."

"Oh, that's okay. Let me introduce Splint," smiled Larry, looking upbeat. "Splint, meet Debbie."

"Hi, Splint," waved Debbie, wondering why Larry seemed so different from earlier.

Splint stood up and shook her hand eagerly. "How do you do Debbie!"

She was surprised at the formal introduction. "How do you do," and finally got her hand back.

Larry could not wait to tell Debbie what they had just thought of. "Splint's new to the tree this year and guess what, he thinks my brother might still be out there, waiting in the box."

Not wanting to give Debbie the impression it was *all* his idea, Splint began explaining. "Well, I wasn't trying to—"

"*What...! Still in the box...!*" interrupted Debbie. She anxiously looked back at Larry, wondering what she was going to hear next.

"Yeah!" continued Larry. "They could have just not seen him when they were taking everyone out... I mean there's so much tissue paper in there, he could have easily been hidden underneath some, couldn't he...?"

"*Larry!*" sighed Debbie, wondering what other crazy ideas this Splint character had put into Larry's head. "What are you saying? That you go out to the box and find out...?"

"Yeah, why not?" answered Larry, clearly looking for her approval.

"Larry... you know Tree-Lord forbids it," complained Debbie, totally shocked by the idea. "It's against the laws of the Elders, you know that?"

"Yeah, I know but—"

"He won't allow you to go out there," she said, pointing out into the room. "He just won't. Nobody's allowed. *Everyone knows that*," and turned to Splint, who just sat there. "*Including you*. I know you're new here, but it was clearly mentioned in the carnival song!"

"I don't care. I'll say I was still sleeping through the song," insisted Splint. "If you want, I'll go find the box for you Larry."

"*What...!*" freaked Debbie. "Why in the land of pine would *you* want to go out there for him?" asked Debbie in frustration, "No offense, but you don't even know him!"

"*Debbie...!*" interrupted Larry, embarrassed by her rudeness. "Let it go, will you please?" and turned to Splint. "Thanks Splint, but no. He's *my* brother and I don't want anyone else getting lost or into trouble over my business. I simply couldn't have that."

"It's no trouble at all, Larry," reassured Splint. "I'm more than glad to help. He's your family after all." Splint climbed to his feet. "So I'm ready when you are."

Debbie spoke slowly and to the point. "Are you really seriously thinking about this, Larry...?" pointing again out into the darkness. "You're *really* thinking of going out there?"

"I have to!" pleaded Larry, hoping she would understand. "I have to try and find out what happened to him. I'm just going crazy here."

Debbie started to panic. Not only did she not understand why Splint was so eager to help Larry, but why Larry would entertain such a crazy notion without the first idea of what was lurking out there, or where the box even was, for that matter. He would either get caught and be in deep trouble with Tree-Lord, or even worse, get himself into unimaginable dangers away from the tree and never make it back.

"Larry!" begged Debbie. "Please don't do this. I don't want to lose you too!"

"You won't lose me, I promise," explained Larry, knowing how concerned she was. "You know I love you, but I have to do this for Terrence!"

Debbie stared back at him, knowing there was nothing more she could say or do to change his mind.

"So where did they take the box?" interrupted Splint. "Does anyone know?"

Larry glanced at Debbie, hoping that if anyone would know, she would. But her eyes had already filled with tears and she turned away in silence, wanting nothing more to do with the idea.

Larry walked slowly over to her. "Debbie, please listen to me," trying to catch her stare. "I know you're concerned, but I have to try and do *something*. I need to keep looking. He's definitely not here on the tree; we've looked everywhere. So he *has* to be out there… *somewhere.*"

Debbie shook her head and said nothing, still adamant her concerns were justified.

Splint jumped in. "So, what's the worst that could happen if the Tree-Lord catches you?" and smiled. "Confine you to the tree?" Larry knew Debbie was not going to be persuaded by anyone, and walked back over to Splint to sort out their plans.

"Right, then. Let's start by trying the room over there," guessed Larry, pointing randomly towards the storage room. "The box might be there. Then if not, maybe we'll try over there." He pointed to the hallway door.

While overhearing Larry's suggestions, Debbie's tears were replaced by a look of disbelief. "What…? The stairs…? You're both seriously going to climb the stairs? Do you even know *how* you're going to climb each step?"

Neither Larry nor Splint knew there were steps through the closed door and looked blankly at one another, then back at Debbie.

Debbie shook her head in frustration, knowing how hopelessly unprepared they both were for the search. "I'll bet you two never thought about the garage, did you?" she blurted out, having no other option but to at least help Larry set off in the right direction.

"The garage?" considered Larry, sounding intrigued.

Debbie rolled her eyes. "Yes! I heard they tend to put the Christmas box in the garage."

Larry once again looked blankly at her.

"Is that through there?" asked Splint, pointing back to the hallway door.

"No," sighed Debbie, shaking her head. "It's through the dining room over there," and pointed to one of two open doors at the other side of the room. "Then it's through the kitchen… I think." She hastily turned away biting her lip, annoyed with herself for helping.

"Right. Through the kitchen to the garage it is then," said Larry. "Now all we have to do is find a way to slip away from here without being noticed." There was another long pause as the two considered this.

"I know!" offered Splint, looking around at all the presents. "How about we just hide between the presents right now, until everyone clibs back to their Bedtime-Branches. Then after they fall asleep, we'll sneak away? It'll be easy!"

"It's a nice idea Splint, but we can't do that," sighed Larry.

"Why not?"

"Well, the lights are usually the last ones to settle into their sockets, and they have an unusual knack of checking to see that everyone is safely hanging from their Bedtime-Branches. It's just too risky."

Debbie noticed that a couple of the lights were already returning back to the tree, as the first signs of morning light crept through the window. "You two better decide quickly," she whispered, "they're coming back." She watched as one of the lights passed close by, then glanced back at Larry and Splint, who were both still looking hopelessly lost for ideas.

VIII

The Plan

EBBIE KNEW THEY WOULD NOT GET ANYWHERE without her help. An idea popped into her head and she felt compelled to share it. "Okay! I don't think I should be saying this," she warned, taking a quick glance around. "In fact, I know I shouldn't be, but what about this..." and leaned in closer to Larry and Splint.

"Okay, tomorrow night, Christmas Eve, you wait until after the family has left the milk and cake out for Santa and have gone to bed. We all know we have to stay asleep on the tree until Santa has come and gone. That also includes Tree-Lord and the Army-Lights, right?"

"Yes, we know that," said Larry, wanting her to get to the plan.

"The only tricky thing," continued Debbie, "is that Santa Claus usually arrives at different times each and every year, depending on the weather conditions, and we know even he's not allowed to see us moving—"

Larry interrupted again, seeing another Army-Light pass by. "Yes, this is all great Debbie, we know this, but what are you thinking?"

"Well, if you're able to wake as soon as the family goes to bed, it gives you a small window of opportunity to get away from the tree, before everyone else wakes up."

Before Larry and Splint could digest the idea, Debbie began retracting it. "No, it's…it's just too dangerous." Worried there were just too many things that could go wrong. "You'd have to climb all the way down without anyone hearing you, which is a feat in and of itself, and facing the wrath of Tree-Lord if you get caught, simply doesn't bear thinking about."

"Really?" pondered Larry, digesting the thought.

"Sounds like a great plan to me!" clapped Splint. "Come on Larry. Like I said earlier, what's the worst he could do if we get caught? Just confine us here to the tree, which we are anyway."

"I don't know what Tree-Lord would do," answered Debbie, nervously fiddling her fingers. "I don't remember anyone ever going outside the perimeter; no one's ever needed to."

"To be honest, I doubt anyone will even notice we've gone," considered Larry, shaking his head, "and Debbie, if anyone does notice, you could maybe try and make something up to distract them until we get back. Couldn't you?"

Debbie paused a moment, as a million thoughts rushed

through her head. "I'm coming with you!"

"What…? Really?!" exclaimed Larry, looking both surprised and concerned. "But—"

"But nothing," interrupted Debbie. "I'm not going to just wait here for you. I'll go totally out of my mind. Whatever we do, we're doing it together… I'm not leaving your side… not now… not ever!"

"But what about Tree-Lord?" asked Larry. "What if…?"

"We'll face him together," nodded Debbie. "Both of us."

Splint jumped into the conversation. "And as long as you're back before they put the tree away, you should be fine. No harm done?" Rubbing his hands together, he kept the momentum going. "Okay then! It's decided, we're going to give it a go, yeah?"

Larry nodded in agreement, mumbling, "Yeah, but we can't get caught. I really don't want to deal with Tree-Lord." He looked out into the dark living room, thinking of his brother. "I hope Terrence is okay out there. I hope we can find him…"

Debbie looked down at Larry and put a hand on his shoulder, still worried about how all this would eventually turn out.

"Hold on a minute…" said Splint, going over the plan in his head. "About this Santa Claus fellow who's going to visit us. What does he look like?"

Debbie looked at him in astonishment. "You've never heard of Santa Claus? You've never heard of the magical man?"

"Yeah, of course I've heard of him, but I don't know what he looks like!" replied Splint, feeling a little awkward.

"Okay, let me show you," smiled Debbie, and she searched the branches above them. "There he is," she whispered, spotting a particular dweller pulling on some pine needles. "Mr. Cringle!" called Debbie. *"Mr. Cringle...!"* The character glanced down at them.

"It's Barry...!" huffed the character, who was a characterized spitting image of Santa Claus. "How many times do I have to tell you all? And he's way, way, bigger too... and fatter for that matter!" As Barry shuffled his way through the branches away from them, Debbie smiled fondly to him, to show she meant no harm or disrespect.

Debbie heard Larry giggling under his hat, and she smiled. She was glad she could still make him laugh with all he was going through. She gently placed a hand on his shoulder and he briefly glanced up. As quick as the glance was, she realized his sounds were not of giggles, but of tears. She tried keeping her own emotions in check and bent down. She lifted back his hat and gently kissed him on his forehead, then looked in his glazed eyes and softly whispered, "Come on you... Let's all go find that brother of yours."

"Hey, you guys, they're all coming back," interrupted Splint, noticing that the circle of Army-Lights around the tree were now returning.

"Yes, we'd better get back up and onto our branches," agreed Debbie, glancing out of the living room window. "It's going to be light soon."

"So?" shrugged Splint, before almost being knocked off his feet by another passing light.

"You mean to say you don't know?" asked Debbie, looking surprised.

"Know what?" asked Splint, looking out at the dawn sky for

clues to what she was talking about.

"Oh… wow, you really don't know, do you…? Sorry, Splint, I thought you were joking," replied Debbie, helping Larry to his feet. "You see the light… the light out there through the window. Well, it comes back every cycle to send us back to sleep, turning us back to our solid state, for the day."

Splint stared out through the window, as it was now light enough to see how much fresh snow had built up overnight, laying heavy on the tree, like toothpaste on a brush. "Oh… That's why!" replied Splint, thinking to himself. "I wondered why I'd woken up without remembering where I'd fallen asleep. It's as sudden as that?"

"It sure is," nodded Debbie.

Larry tapped them both on the shoulder. "Come on. We'd best get back up and get ready." They all started climbing up the tree, along with the remaining Army-Lights returning from the final shift of the night.

As they climbed, Splint glanced back down to the bottom of the tree and noticed one of the lights hopping around amongst the presents, checking the area before jumping back into the tree. "Hey, Larry," whispered Splint, "you were right about them checking."

Larry looked down. "Yeah, there's not much that they miss. Efficient as ever!" then glanced at Debbie, hoping their new plan would be good enough to fool even the lights.

The conversation went quiet, as the worry of what dangers lay ahead of them away from the tree, began to take hold.

Suddenly, and seemingly from out of nowhere, Darrel and his wife Sydney appeared. "Hey, there! So we finally found you!" smiled Sydney, a crème-white porcelain Christmas bell, with a delicate blue bow wrapped around her waist.

"Yeah… where were you all for the 'Pine-Party'?" inquired Darrel. "We missed you!" then noticed Larry's brother was not with them. "And where's your brother gotten to?"

Larry's face dropped and he shook his head. "We still haven't found him."

Darrel smiled. "You're kidding, right…?" His face dropped quickly as he noticed how serious Debbie and Larry were. "Wow, Terrence eh!"

Larry stepped over to Darrel and whispered, "We can trust you, yeah?"

"Yes, of course you can, Larry."

"We're leaving the tree tomorrow to find him."

"What!" gasped Darrel, not believing his ears. "When?"

"Right after the family goes to bed," answered Larry. "Just before the visit."

"*Leaving…!* What do you mean *leaving?*" stuttered Darrel, looking dumbfounded. "You mean *out there?*" pointing out into the living room. "Larry! Are you mad?"

Darrel glanced at Debbie, while quickly thinking of a way to talk some sense into them. "Come on, Larry! You know these things just happen. Everyone knows that. It's upsetting, but it's something we come to terms with!"

"Yeah, I've heard that from everyone else too," sighed Larry, as Splint, listening from a couple of branches away, turned his back to keep out of the conversation.

"Obviously Tree-Lord doesn't know about this?" whispered Darrel, with concern.

"No! And it needs to stay that way too," hushed Larry, carefully glancing around.

"Of course, Larry, but sooner or later he'll know you've all gone," warned Darrel.

"We'd be happy with later!" interrupted Splint from above their heads, then continued climbing up and away to his branch.

"Who was that?" asked Darrel, feeling rudely interrupted.

"His name's Splint," smiled Larry. "He's okay," and put a hand on Darrel's shoulder. "We need to get to bed now."

Darrel understood Larry had already made his decision and it was pointless taking it any further.

"Hey!" called Darrel, as Larry turned away. "I guess you'll need these then," and threw Larry a sack full of fresh pine needles.

"What are all these for…?"

"I picked them for the 'Pine-Party' earlier," replied Darrel. "But… Well," and looked a little awkward. "Well… You know."

Larry did not know what to say and stared at the sack. Debbie smiled, knowing how much the gesture meant to Larry. It would have taken them far longer than they had left before daylight, to find and pick even a small handful of fresh pines off the tree.

Darrel sniffed and whispered, "So Larry, you probably know… But sucking the needles this close to bedtime, can help keep you awake a bit longer…" and stopped abruptly, as another Army-Light passed by. They all stood there, looking as casual as possible until the light had passed out of earshot. It settled back into its light socket waiting for the fresh charge later in the day, when they would be switched on again.

Larry looked back at Darrel. "Yeah… I know that, but why

are you…?"

Darrel patiently waited for the glow from the Army-Light to fade, until he was sure it was fast asleep. He pulled Larry in close and whispered, "Yeah, but did you know that the fresher ones can also make you sleep lighter too. So it might help you make that *early start* you were looking for. I came across that fact when I was thinking of going out there myself… A long time ago now mind you, when Old-Billy went missing. But I ended up not having the," and paused a moment. "Anyway, who knows where he went to." He then cleared his throat and smiled. "The rest in the sack should help you on the journey."

Larry pulled the sack in close and smiled, still too overwhelmed to say anything. He placed a hand on Darrel's shoulder then turned and climbed up and away, along with Debbie, to prepare for the journey ahead.

IX

Risking It All

HE SMELL OF THE TRADITIONAL CHRISTMAS EVE dinner of sausage rolls, salad greens and plum pudding lingered in the house, long after the meal was finished. Aaron and Emma were playing in the living room while Dad cleaned the kitchen. Mom had quietly disappeared upstairs to the bedroom, away from the children.

Aaron was leaning on the window ledge, his chin resting on his hands, staring out at the falling snow. "What if it doesn't stop snowing? Do you still think he'll be able to find our house?" he asked, looking out at what used to resemble the front garden.

The garden was now just part of a collection of white mounds that blended in and out of one another, stretching across the snow covered street. Tire tracks made earlier in the day were now completely covered, and the snow-laden trees that lined each side of the street revealed only a hint to the road hidden underneath.

"We might have to leave the Christmas tree lights on, so he can find our house. Don't you think, Emma... Emma?" Aaron noticed his sister was kneeling under the Christmas tree, gently shaking the colorfully wrapped presents. Aaron giggled and quickly ran over to join her under the tree. Suddenly they heard footsteps walking down the stairs.

"Quickly...! Quickly!" giggled Aaron, getting up and running over to the couch. Emma dropped the present and scurried over to join Aaron, but on standing she knocked a tree branch and one of the decorations dropped off its Bedtime-Branch onto the branch below.

She glanced over and noticed that some of the decorations were still swinging, but, hoping no one would notice, she quickly looked back at the television just as Mom entered from the hallway.

"*Love!*" called Mom through to the kitchen. "I've finished most of them," then glanced at the children staring intently at the television.

"Wow, that was quick...! It would have taken me till midnight!" answered Dad, walking in from the kitchen. "Okay then, come on kids," clapping his hands. "Let's get you both tucked in for bed."

Aaron and Emma sulked, as they had done the night before, and the night before that. "Oh, just a few more minutes, Mom?" huffed Emma, crossing her arms.

"Yeah, it's Christmas Eve. Oh please, Dad?" sighed Aaron, backing up his sister.

"Oh nothing! Now come on you two," smiled Mom. "The

sooner you both get to sleep, the sooner Santa Claus will come and Christmas Day will arrive."

"Really...?" exclaimed Aaron, wonderment filling his eyes.

"Yes, really!" confirmed Dad. "Now come on, off to bed with you both."

The children jumped off the couch and ran past Mom into the hallway. "Mom, are we going to leave the tree lights on for Santa tonight?" asked Aaron. "He'll need them to find our house in all that snow!"

"Yes, can we Mom? Oh please?" said Emma, taking a last look at the tree on the way out of the door.

"He has Rudolph's nose to guide him," explained Mom with a smile, and followed them out into the hallway.

"Wow, it's that bright...?"

"Yes, of course," answered Dad. "I mean how else would he find his way around in all this snowy weather!" He glanced a smile to Mom as they climbed the stairs. "It's so bright, it actually shines in through the window, so Santa can see just fine without our lights!"

"Oh, did we leave a mince pie and some milk out for Santa, Dad?" asked Aaron.

"Yes, son," said Dad. "It'll all be down there waiting for him when he arrives, don't you worry," and led them upstairs to bed.

Later that night, Mom and Dad were relaxing next to one another on the sofa, roasting chestnuts in front of the warm fireplace. 'Silent Night' played softly on the radio. The tree lights warmed the room and the holiday smell of tree pine and roasted chestnuts hung in the air. They had finished wrapping the last few presents and were now relaxing with a festive glass of wine.

Over at the brightly lit tree, Splint carefully opened an eye and looked over at Mr. and Mrs. Ferguson cracking open their tasty treats. He glanced at Larry who was also worriedly aware that the two were staying up far later than either of them had expected. They knew that every minute Mr. and Mrs. Ferguson stayed up, meant one less minute they had to escape from the tree before Santa Claus arrived.

"What are they doing?" asked Splint, nervously.

"Be quiet!" hushed Larry, glancing around the branches, worried someone would hear them. Splint sighed impatiently and they both stared back out into the room, desperately hoping Mom and Dad would retire off to bed shortly.

"Another drop of wine, dear?" offered Dad, lifting the bottle.

"Oh go on then, just a drop more. It is Christmas after all!" giggled Mom, showing her glass.

Larry sighed quietly, knowing full well they were going to be in for a longer wait.

Finally, when it seemed they would never retire, Dad got to his feet and stretched his arms out, yawning, "Ooh…! Okay, I think I'm ready for bed. I'm bushed, love," and patted his unusually large stomach from over indulging on dinner, pudding and chestnuts. "You coming?"

"Yes, I'm tired too!" agreed Mom, getting to her feet. "Those were tasty chestnuts," and made her way over to the hallway door. "We'll have to take some with us for New Year's Eve."

Dad switched off the radio and placed the guard in front of the open fireplace, then repositioned the Christmas stockings that were hanging from their hooks, still waiting to be filled. He yawned his way over to the hallway door, then closed it gently behind him, and they both quietly climbed the stairs to bed.

Over at the tree, Larry and Splint opened their eyes, looking relieved to finally see them leave.

"Oh no!" murmured Larry, as he stopped trying to climb down from his branch.

"What's the matter...?" whispered Splint, before noticing the Army-Lights were still switched on. Mom and Dad had forgotten to switch them off. "So what do we do...?"

Before Larry could reply, the hallway door suddenly swung back open. "Goodness me. We almost forgot the lights," laughed Dad, walking hastily over to the tree.

Larry and Splint instinctively snapped back into their solid states, though they were still swinging slightly from their branches.

"I'd lose my head if it wasn't screwed on," continued Dad, switching the lights off and unplugging the cord from the wall. "We don't want a fire on the tree now do we, especially on Christmas Eve..." He chuckled. "I mean, where would Santa put all the Christmas presents *then?*"

Mom laughed at his remark and they took a last look around the room to check everything had been attended to, then closed the door behind them. Their footsteps faded up the stairs, leaving the room in silence.

The streetlight shone back into the darkened room from the front window as Splint and Larry opened their eyes once again. They checked to see that the coast was clear before quietly lifting themselves down off their Bedtime-Branches.

Debbie arrived, carrying Tinsel in her arms. "Hi, guys," she whispered. "I didn't think they'd ever go off to bed," and passed Tinsel over to Larry. "Now do we all have everything?"

Splint quietly tapped the filled pine sack hanging over his shoulder and nodded. Larry tapped his pine sack too, while settling Tinsel under his arm.

"Great! Now let's get down before he arrives," whispered Splint, leading the way, followed hastily by Debbie and then Larry.

"Remember what we said earlier Splint," warned Debbie.

"Yeah, I remember," replied Splint, pointing to the trunk of the tree. "Keep close to the center of the tree, where there's less chance of us waking anyone, cuz the branches don't shake there... Easy-peasy...!"

"Yeah, but let's be careful, though, okay?" whispered Larry.

"Hold on a minute," considered Debbie, carefully dropping onto the next branch. "Can someone remind me why we decided not to climb down the back of the tree." She looked up at Larry. "Didn't you say there was no one back there?"

"Yes, there isn't," confirmed Larry. "But the branches were far too brittle and thin. We'd all fall before we got anywhere near the bottom."

"Oh, that's right!" nodded Debbie. "I remember now."

Larry looked down and noticed Splint had already gotten three or four branches ahead of them. "Hey, Debbie," he whispered. "We'd better try and keep up. He's pretty nimble, isn't he!"

Debbie was equally surprised to see how far down Splint had

gotten and seemed to be ever quickening his pace.

"Hey, Splint!" whispered Debbie, as loud as she dared. Splint looked up. "Sorry, but could you hold on for a minute? We're not as fast as you!"

While Splint waited for the group to catch up, he tried estimating how much further they had to cover before Santa's imminent arrival, by looking down to the presents then across the darkened room to the open door of the dining room.

Debbie and Larry continued their way quietly down through the sleeping tree towards Splint, trying to be as careful as possible not to shake any of the branches.

Debbie could not help but feel she was the one holding up the group. Having small hoof-like feet, she was having great difficulty gripping the slippery wooden branches. She tried quickening her pace, but stepped a little too quickly and slipped awkwardly on a branch, causing it to shake.

Everyone froze and watched

helplessly as the strong ripple worked its way down to the very tip of the branch, where the sound of a little bell broke the silence.

'Ding-a-ling!'

They all held their breath, expecting the worst.

X

Keeping Up

HMOMENT HAD PASSED and they heard nothing. Debbie glanced up at Larry, who was still expecting to hear the sound of a Tree-Dweller, or see an Army-Light appear, investigating the disturbance.

Luckily there was not a sound from anywhere, just the crackle of cooling embers in the fireplace.

They breathed a sigh of relief.

"I'm so sorry," whispered Debbie, planting her foot securely down on the next branch.

"It's okay," whispered Larry from above. "Just take your time and really try feeling those branches with your feet." Larry was having problems of his own, as Tinsel had decided he wanted to climb down himself through the branches, and was wriggling around under Larry's arm. Meanwhile, Splint continued to plan the easiest way down through the branches, keeping as far away as possible from the sleeping dwellers.

After descending a couple more branches, Splint found himself at a point where the thickest branch to step on was too low to reach. He stepped to the side to try a somewhat thinner branch that was easier to reach.

He carefully stepped down with one foot, gently testing his weight on the thinner branch. It seemed fine. He had just taken his weight off the other foot when '*crack!*', the thin branch snapped from under him and he fell.

Splint grabbed frantically in all directions, and managed to catch the needles of a passing branch. The resulting force jolted his body and flicked the pine sack from his shoulder and off his arm. With a final gasp, he caught the strap with the end of his fingertips just above a sleeping dweller, the same dweller that Emma knocked off its branch earlier that evening when running from the tree.

Splint breathed a sigh of relief as the sack swung back and forth in front of the dweller's face. He carefully pulled the sack up and this time lifted it over his head and shoulder, then signaled to Larry and Debbie that everything was fine. Slowly and a little more carefully, Splint stepped around the sleeping dweller and continued down onto the next branch.

Larry noticed that he was holding his sack in the same precarious way Splint had been, and quickly adjusted it to avoid any further scares. He tapped it and nodded to Debbie that it was secure. It was at that moment that he realized he had forgotten his Tree-Umbrella and began to panic, as though his whole 'tree-dom' was about to fall in around him. Everyone knew he never went anywhere without his umbrella and now he felt in need of it more than ever.

"Psss...! Hey, Debbie...!" whispered Larry. "I have to go back up," and held Tinsel out to her.

Debbie looked confused. "What...? Are you joking? Go back...! What are you talking about?"

Larry began stuttering nervously. "I... I... forgot my u- um- umbrella! It's up th- there on my b- b- branch. I won't be a minute, I promise," and scanned the branches for the quickest return.

Debbie grabbed his foot as it lifted off the branch. "Are you out of your flippin' mind?" she whispered, amazed he was actually thinking of returning to his Bedtime-Branch. "You don't need the umbrella. You've already gotten this far without it," she argued.

With a nervous look on his face, Larry took a moment to think.

"I promise you Larry, you don't need it," begged Debbie. "Now please, come on... Let's get down from here, before he arrives."

Larry took a deep breath and glanced up into the thick branches. He really did not know what to do and looked at Tinsel, then back at Debbie. Taking another deep breath, he tucked Tinsel back under his arm and continued slowly descending through the branches.

Debbie and Larry finally found themselves at the bottom of the tree, where Splint was anxiously waiting, eager to get across the living room floor to the dining room.

"Okay, are we ready? Come on!" beckoned Splint. "Let's keep moving as quickly as we can." He noticed Larry looking a little out of breath. "Is everyone okay…?"

"Yeah…" panted Larry, placing Tinsel on the floor, then stretched out his back. "Yeah, we're good… We're fine."

"Okay! Let's go then!" nodded Splint, and quickly ran as quietly as he could across the living room floor towards the dining room.

Larry watched Splint pace on ahead, while Debbie gazed out across the rest of the room. For the first time in her life she saw the whole room from the bottom of the tree, without any sign of an Army-Light to guard her. This gave her a strange and worrying feeling. They *really* were alone down there and from this point onwards there was no looking back. She looked at Larry. "You ready to do this then…?"

Although nervous too, Larry nodded eagerly and smiled, looking forward to finally finding his brother. "Right then! Let's be off…!" whispered Debbie, and she took a deep breath before sprinting off towards Splint.

Larry trotted after her and stole a glance back up through the branches, still feeling uneasy about leaving his umbrella in the tree. Not looking where he was going, he carelessly caught his foot on the lighting cable running from the wall socket into the tree, sending a small vibration up through the dense branches.

He stood still, looking worryingly down at his foot, then across to Splint and Debbie, who were now well ahead of him. Even Tinsel, who was usually by his side, had already caught up with Splint. "Wait," whispered Larry across the floor, but they were too far away to hear him.

He glanced back into the tree to see if he could see any

movement or flickering lights, but luckily all seemed calm. He noticed the tree was extra large this year and still looked magical even with everyone fast asleep. Catching himself gazing at the tree, he realized he had no time to waste. He quickly stepped over the cable, and ran as fast as he could to catch up with the others.

High up in the tree however, two lights had woken up and were flashing to one another. They quietly jumped from their sockets and quickly made their way down through the tree towards the bottom, to investigate the vibration.

In the meantime, Larry and the group sped across the wooden floor towards the dining room door, fully aware of Santa's imminent arrival. They could not help but occasionally glance back at the tree to reassure themselves no one had woken up, then out through the frosted windows to see if they could spot 'Him' coming.

Larry noticed something from the corner of his eye and glanced out through the window, just in time to see two rows of brightly colored lights disappear through the snowy sky. He heard a *'thump'* as something heavy landed on the rooftop.

"Oh, goodness me," gasped Debbie. *"It's him already! We're not going to make it!"*

"Keep going!" exclaimed Larry, *"Don't look back!"*

Back at the tree, one of the lights had finally arrived near the bottom, and looking out, it noticed Larry scampering towards the dining room. The Army-Light emitted a bright glow, then flashed erratically in a panic as the second light arrived.

Another bang from the rooftop echoed through the house, startling the two lights. They scurried up the tree and jumped back into their sockets.

Just as their lights went out, a bright flash of light and sparkling dust illuminated the whole living room.

XI

The Empty Bedtime-Branches

EAVY BOOTS STEPPED ACROSS the living room floor. "Ho… ho… ho…!" laughed a very happy Santa Claus. His red coat, trimmed in white, contrasted with his shiny black leather belt and boots. He walked over to the tree where he dropped the red sack off his shoulder onto the floor next to him and knelt down. "Okay, Aaron and Emma," he chuckled, unrolling the very long list from his hand. "What am I leaving you this year?" He scanned down the long list of names with his pudgy finger until he found them both. He chuckled again opening the red sack and began rummaging around inside, just as Splint and Tinsel made it behind the dining room door into safety.

As Santa pulled a big present from the sack, he accidentally knocked the tree and swung the sleeping dwellers wildly on their

Bedtime-Branches. He placed the present under the tree and put his hands back in the sack. "Oh, they *have* been good again this year!" and he pulled out an even bigger present.

Splint looked back into the living room and waved his arm at Debbie and Larry to hurry them up.

Luckily, Santa was still too busy pulling out even more presents from his sack to notice, as Debbie and Larry finally made it past Splint and fell behind the door, exhausted, but relieved.

Tinsel wagged his tail wildly and jumped all over Larry, playfully licking his face. "Oh, stop it, Tinsel," giggled Larry, "you know it tickles!"

Splint looked back over at Santa and could not help but stare in amazement at the magical man in his big red coat. "Wow..." he whispered, smiling.

The final present was pulled out of the sack, trailed by sparkling pixie-dust that again lit up the room. Santa slowly got up and turned around, which immediately brought Splint out of his daze and he jumped quickly behind the door to hide with the others.

Santa Claus chuckled to himself. "Peek-a-boo! You there!"

Splint stood still, looking worried, wondering if Santa was speaking to him.

Larry, who was still lying down and catching his breath, looked up and whispered, "Hey! He didn't see you just then, did he?"

"Um... I'm not sure," answered Splint, still dazed from finally seeing the great Santa Claus. "I don't think so..."

From behind the door, they all noticed a blast of bright light and sparkling fairy dust, and then the living room quickly fell back into darkness. They listened intently to the sound of Santa's boots walking across the roof. His sled lifted off and away, back into the snowy sky, not to return again for another year. The house was left in complete and utter silence.

Splint, Larry and Debbie looked at one another and began to reflect on what they had just done. They giggled with nervous relief at how close they came to being caught by the one and only Santa Claus. If they had left just one minute later, it would have been impossible to get away from the tree.

Splint was the first to recover himself from the giddy excitement. He carefully glanced back through the doorway to check on the tree. "Okay, come on. We'd better start moving!" he whispered. "They'll be waking shortly."

The smiles dropped off Larry and Debbie's faces, as they realized this was only the start of their journey, a serious journey, filled with unknown dangers. Their plan to get away from the tree was now a reality.

Splint helped Larry and Debbie to their feet and looked into the dining room. "Come on, let's get moving," he whispered, tentatively making his way into the room. Debbie grabbed Larry's hand tightly and they followed.

"Ooh…" gasped Larry, stopping abruptly.

"Are you okay?" asked Debbie.

"Yeah, I just got a twinge in my foot, but I'm all right," smiled Larry, squeezing her hand reassuringly. They both set off to catch up with Splint.

Back at the tree, everyone was waking up and voices were calling out to one another.

"He's been, he's been...!"

"Look, everyone! Look at all the presents!"

At the top of the tree, the two lights were already flashing frantically to Tree-Lord. "Hold on... Hold on a minute!" demanded Tree-Lord. "A little slower if you could!"

The lights calmed down and blinked a little more slowly, one at a time.

Tree-Lord nodded as he quietly watched, listening intently to what they had to say, then his face dropped like a stone. "What...? Left the tree, you say!" and glanced urgently out into the room. *"When...? Are you both sure?"*

The lights flashed again, confirming their story.

Tree-Lord quickly cleared his throat and interrupted the increasing commotion below him. "Excuse me everyone, is Larry down there...?"

A voice in the middle of the tree called back, "His umbrella's down here, hanging from his Bedtime-Branch. So he must be around here somewhere your Lordship! Hey, Larry...! Larry, where are you?"

"Has anybody seen him?" interrupted Tree-Lord.

"Tinsel... Tinsel! Come on, boy!" called another voice, helping the search. "No. He's not here either, your Lordship... Maybe Debbie knows?"

The muttering from the tree got noticeably louder.

"Larry never goes anywhere without his Tree-Umbrella!"

"Well maybe he fell into Santa's sack!"

"What, Larry and Tinsel? Surely not both of 'em!"

Tree-Lord called above the chatter, *"Debbie...! Debbie! Is Larry there with you...?"* but there was no reply. Tree-Lord loudly cleared his throat to silence all the muttering. "Does anyone here know where they've gone?"

Everyone stared up at him in silence.

"Come on, someone must know... anyone?" sighed Tree-Lord. "Okay then... No one plays in the newly arrived presents until we find out where they've gone." His remark was met with sighs from everyone. "Well, do yourselves and our missing dwellers a favor then and come forward to help them!"

Everyone looked blankly at one another, wondering if someone would come forward.

A quiet voice broke the silence. "I know where they went!" Gasps echoed through the branches. Darrel's wife Sydney nervously appeared from behind a branch, shrugging off Darrel who was trying in vain to prevent her from stepping into the spotlight.

"No Sydney, we promised!" whispered Darrel frantically.

"Good... Good," smiled Tree-Lord, bending over in his socket to get a better look at who he was talking to. "Thank you Sydney. Where did they go?"

Sydney looked up and noticed a calm yet concerned look on Tree-Lord's face. "We promised not to say anything your Lordship, but I'm so concerned for them out there," replied Sydney, nervously rubbing her hands. "You understand, don't you?"

"Yes, of course I do. We're all concerned for them. But please, Sydney, time is precious. Where did they go?" Tree-Lord's patience showed signs of thinning.

Sydney was still more than a little hesitant about speaking up, and stole a glance back at Darrel, who was shaking his head at her. Knowing it was too late now, and finding it difficult to swallow with her drying mouth, she took a deep breath and turned back to Tree-Lord. "We spoke to them before the sleep, your Lordship. Larry's gone out to look for his brother, who's been missing since we all woke up from the box."

Tree-Lord's face dropped and he interrupted. "You said *them!* So Debbie's gone with him too…! Anyone else?"

"Um… Yes," replied Sydney, "Obviously Tinsel. Oh, and a new dweller too, but I don't know his name your Lordship." She bowed her head in respect.

Tree-Lord's face turned red with anger, and he briefly shook the upper half of the tree in his frustration, before calming himself down to address his bewildered dwellers. "Larry and his brother have both been with us all for a very long time now, as many of you know. They are among the kindest and most loving members of our family *anyone* could wish to have... *However*," continued Tree-Lord sternly, "Larry knows, as we *all* do, that it's not for us to decide who returns to enjoy life on the tree each year. And, my fellow dwellers, *that* is why we celebrate it so fully. Breaking these laws with a curiosity for answers that have already been so fully explained by our forefathers, not only puts him and his inquisitive friends in danger, but puts our whole way of life on the tree in danger, too."

Sydney dropped her head and walked slowly back to Darrel, who sighed in disbelief, wondering how much damage she had just done to Larry's plan.

Everyone on the tree began chatting about Tree-Lord's

speech.

Tree-Lord again cleared his throat to silence the crowd. "So it looks as though we are missing a few of our friends, our closest friends. Whether they left to find a brother, or to spend time alone to reflect on their loss, is not for me to say. *But,*" and paused a moment to choose his words carefully. "But as stated by our forefathers for the safety of everyone here in the family, we are *never...* I repeat *never,* to venture outside the protected area."

He paused again to let the crowd digest his comment.

"So I say to my army of brave lights... Go! Go and find our strayed members! Protect them from harm and bring them back home to safety!"

The Tree-Dwellers cheered at his decision, while Tree-Lord turned to his head Army-Light and began blinking to it, informing it of his orders.

Before long, a squadron of Army-Lights made their way down off the tree. The dwellers, totally overwhelmed by the heart-warming effort Tree-Lord was making, waved down and across the floor to the brave lights as they set off in search of Larry and the group.

XII

Fragile Things

PLINT, LARRY, DEBBIE AND TINSEL were carefully making their way through the dining room, staying as close as they could to the walls and side furniture. The room was particularly dark, especially with the thick red curtains drawn across the windows.

They did notice the outline of four chairs placed in the center of the room around a large oak dining table. From one end of the table to the other lay a burgundy cloth runner with tassels at either end, and on top of the runner was fresh holly, wrapped around several festive candles.

The group found themselves below the hand crafted wall cabinet at the side of the room, that proudly held the white bone china that was a wedding gift from the Ferguson's grandparents many years ago. "I can't see anything in here, can you?" asked Splint, hopelessly feeling his way through the darkness.

"Just keep moving straight," suggested Debbie, and bumped into the back of Larry. "Ooh! Sorry!" Suddenly a light switched on and they all crouched down.

Unknown to them, their movements had triggered the sensor light that was plugged in at the bottom of the wall across the room. It shone a soft blue light across the room. They stayed perfectly still, wondering who else was in the room with them.

"Stay boy!" whispered Larry, noticing that Tinsel wanted to run over to the light. They glanced worryingly around. Strangely enough, there did not seem to be anyone around and they could not hear anything either.

"What do we do?" whispered Larry.

"Just stay still," hushed Splint, listening carefully for any sounds. To everyone's surprise the blue light switched itself off.

"They must have gone, whoever it was," sighed Splint, standing up, and he took a step forward. His movements immediately switched the blue night-light on again, causing Splint to stop mid-step. "Who's doing that?" he huffed, becoming increasingly frustrated at not making any headway through the room.

"I don't like this at all," cautioned Larry, and gently grabbed Debbie's hand.

Again, after what seemed like an eternity to the dwellers, the light *'clicked'* and switched itself off. They all stayed perfectly still in the darkness, nervous and even more confused.

"Okay, let's just stay still for a bit longer to make sure they've finally left," whispered Splint.

A little more time passed in the darkness and as nothing happened, Debbie was ready to give it another go. She cautiously took a small step forward.

The blue light switched on again.

"Oh, I don't believe this," muttered Debbie. "Who's doing that?"

Splint's eyes lit up. "Hold on, it might be one of those lights that wakes up when they sense something's moving. They're really light sleepers, you know."

"What?" whispered Debbie.

"Yeah, they're usually there to help when you're stranded in the dark."

"Really...? You sure?" whispered Larry, looking over to the light.

"Yeah, I think so. There was one in the shop where I came from. And besides, I can't see anyone else around here, can you?" shrugged Splint, and he looked up through the lit room to prove his point. "And we're never going to get to the garage if we just take a step every ten 'ticks' now, will we!"

Larry knew Splint had a point. They really needed to get down into the garage, hopefully before daylight. They had already spent far too long standing around in the dining room, and if Debbie's plan of the house was right, they still had to get through the kitchen.

Splint took a bold step forward in the softly lit room, wondering what would happen. Nothing did, and he continued to take another step, then another.

Larry and Debbie sighed with relief and carefully followed

Splint through the room that was now kindly lit by the blue light.

Splint would regularly pull ahead of them, taking it upon himself to check that the coast was clear before the rest ventured out into the open. Larry and Debbie were finding it hard to keep up with his ambitious pace.

All of a sudden Larry moaned loudly and grabbed Debbie's arm to steady himself.

"What's the matter, Larry? Are you okay?" asked Debbie.

"Yes, I'm fine," replied Larry, trying to carry on.

Debbie noticed he was limping slightly on one foot and tugged on his arm to stop. "Hey! What's the matter with your foot…?"

Larry tried smiling. "Nothing, I'm okay! I… I just fell on it earlier when we were running from the tree." He looked away, trying to dismiss her concerns. "I'm fine, nothing to worry about, honest."

Debbie could read Larry like a book. She knew he was playing it down, so she grabbed his arm again before he could set off. "Let me see it!"

"It's okay!" dismissed Larry again.

"So let me see it then!"

He sighed, looking ahead to check that Splint was far enough away not to see, then leaned up against the wall and lifted his foot.

Straining in the dull blue light, Debbie noticed Larry's foot was badly cracked and had a triangular piece clearly missing from the heel. She tried to contain her concerns, but now had grave doubts about them being able to make it any further. "Does it *really hurt?*"

"No, it just stings a bit now and then," answered Larry, still playing down the seriousness of his injury. "Look, don't worry! I can stand on it... Look!" He stood up. "Really... It just... stings a bit."

"*Stings a bit!*" freaked Debbie. "You're kidding me, aren't you. A chip *that* big... Where's your missing piece, do you still have it?"

Larry put a hand in his pocket and pulled out the piece of glass. "Don't tell Splint...! He'll want to call it all off."

"Call what off?" smiled Splint, walking back towards them. "Are you both okay...? Why did we stop?" He noticed Larry quickly close his hand.

"What have you got there, Larry?" asked Splint, with the smile dropping from his face.

Larry knew he had not been subtle enough hiding it and reluctantly opened his hand.

"Where's that from?"

Larry glanced at Debbie, then leaned against the wall and lifted his foot.

"How does it feel?" asked Splint, to Larry's surprise. "Can you still walk on it?"

"Yeah, I'm fine... It's just a ... a small chip, no problem."

"Good then," nodded Splint. "So let's keep moving. I really nee— We really need to get to the box as soon as we can, hopefully before light, yeah?" Larry nodded back eagerly and Splint once again walked away briskly ahead of them both.

Debbie looked at Larry. "Did you notice that...?"

"What?" asked Larry, who had not noticed anything out of the ordinary, and was already testing his weight back on his foot.

"Nothing. It doesn't matter," smiled Debbie, forgetting about it. She held Larry's arm to help support his weight. "Are you sure you want to go on? If you want, we can still go back you know? I'm sure they haven't noticed we've gone." She smiled. "Right now they're probably all too busy down amongst all the presents."

"Yeah. I could have had a better start, eh!" considered Larry. "But I'm fine, thanks. We'll keep going and see where it gets us. I'll let you know if it gets worse, I promise," Larry glanced ahead to Splint. "Wow, he's keeping up that pace. Just what we need eh! Come on, Debbie, let's catch up!"

"Yes… Isn't he." Debbie was beginning to feel a little frustration creeping in, at just how far ahead Splint had already gotten in such a short time, knowing full well that Larry was struggling with his injury.

Debbie lifted his big arm over her shoulder and they hurried as best they could to catch up with Splint. All this time Tinsel was keeping close by Larry's side, simply enjoying the long walk his master was taking him on.

Debbie's attempt to help support Larry quickly began to falter, and she found herself struggling with his sheer size and weight.

Splint, meanwhile, was still pushing on ahead, seemingly uninterested in how Larry and Debbie were coping with the pace he was setting.

"He doesn't care at all, does he?" snapped Debbie.

"What's that…?" strained Larry, stepping gently on his damaged foot.

"Well, just look at him go…! He hasn't looked back once to see how we're doing, or if we need his help."

"I kinda wish I hadn't forgotten my umbrella," Larry

admitted, feeling guilty about the situation.

"I thought we were all in this together," sighed Debbie, and at that exact moment, Splint looked back to see where they were.

"Look! There you go!" smiled Larry, nudging her with his elbow. "He's just done it now."

Debbie rolled her eyes in frustration. "Of course, *now* he does it!"

"Oh, come on Debbie, what's the matter with you?" asked Larry. "He's doing exactly what he should be doing, keeping the pace strong. Otherwise we'll never get there!" He kissed her reassuringly on her head.

Debbie was still frustrated by Splint's seeming lack of concern. Maybe he had never been a team player and was just thinking about his *own* safety. That made sense. But on the other hand, if that *was* the case, then why would he be helping them in finding Larry's brother? There was nothing to be gained from it. He could be safely back at the tree, checking out all the presents with everyone else. All these thoughts kept swimming around in her head, until she noticed Larry whistling the 'Carnival Song' from earlier on at the tree. It lifted her away from her thoughts.

Out in front, Splint heard something move behind the door next to him, close to the end of the dining room. He immediately stopped and threw up a hand signal for everyone else to do the same.

Larry stopped whistling and they both stood still.

Splint sneaked quietly over to the edge of the door and carefully poked his head around it to look inside.

Once again the room was dark, but he could make out some shelves that were filled from floor to ceiling with books of all shapes and sizes, and what looked like an armchair and side table at the far end, next to some heavy curtains. He looked back at Larry and Debbie, and placing a finger over his lips, quietly waved them over.

Splint heard the noise again from inside the room and looked back in, trying to find its source.

Larry and Debbie had no sooner arrived at the door, when Tinsel began growling. "Quiet boy!" hushed Larry, squinting into the darkness. "What can you see, Splint…?"

They noticed something scuttle across the floor, briefly followed by a dim flash of light that set Tinsel off growling again. "It's okay, boy," said Larry, carefully picking him up.

"Did you see that?" asked Splint.

"Yeah," whispered Larry, trying to calm Tinsel's shaking.

There was another flash of light, this one bright enough for them to notice what it was.

"An Army-Light!" gasped Larry. "What's it doing all the way out here?"

As they struggled with this new development, they noticed a large, dark shape, jump down from the corner of the room. It was the family cat; its tail swinging wildly across the wooden floor, as it crept slowly and deliberately towards the light.

The light, lying on its side in the middle of the floor, suddenly lit up brightly and jumped to its wiry feet, then scurried towards the bookshelves at the far end of the room. The cat quickly intercepted it, flicking it casually into the air with its paw, as it would a mouse, then watched as it helplessly smacked down onto the floor.

The light fought to get up, but there seemed to be no escape. The cat pounced again, scooping it into its paws and tossing it high into the air. The light flickered as it fell, slamming again onto the hard wooden floor.

Splint, Debbie and Larry stood paralyzed, horrified by the sight. They watched in vain as the cat slowly and methodically drained the remaining life out of the helpless light.

Debbie turned away, hiding her head in her hands, unable to watch any more.

Suddenly, after the light had lay motionless for a moment, it shone brightly and jumped back to its feet. It started to run, making a last ditch effort to escape through a door. *Their* door.

Splint and Larry panicked, realizing they were going to be in serious danger if the cat saw them, but at the same time feeling helpless; it was all happening so fast and they were frozen with terror. All Splint could think of as the light approached the door was to wave his hands around and yell, "*Go back! Go back!*"

As Larry was preparing to accept his fate, the relentless cat scooped the light up with its sharp claws and dragged it helplessly back into the room. With a loud '*hiss*', the cat flicked it into the air once more, and this time swiped the exhausted light much harder, causing it to explode into a million pieces. Sparks flew everywhere, cascading down onto the cat, making it jump and twitch.

Larry, Debbie and Splint stood there silently, rooted to the spot, their mouths gaping open in shock and disbelief. They watched the cat quickly lose interest and stroll casually away, disappearing into the dark at the far end of the room, as if it was never there; leaving the shattered fragments of a dead light discarded all over the floor.

The group stood there in silence for a moment longer, struggling to digest what they had just witnessed: an Army-Light, the strongest thing they knew existed, made to look so defenseless out there in the dangerous world, far away from their tree.

Splint finally turned his attention to Larry, who was thinking exactly the same thing. "We're in deep trouble out here, aren't we?" admitted Splint, trying to swallow with his dry mouth. Larry nodded.

Larry gently pulled Debbie's hands away from her face. "It's gone, Debbie. Debbie... It's okay now." He comforted her in his arms, knowing all too well that they had been lucky to avoid the attentions of the cat, at least for now.

XIII

The Humming

PLINT TOOK A FINAL LOOK at the broken Army-Light, then adjusted the pine-sack hanging from his shoulder. "Come on you two," he whispered, walking swiftly past Larry and Debbie towards the open kitchen door. "We'd better keep moving."

Larry acknowledged him, knowing that Splint was right. If what Debbie heard was correct, then the door at the far end of the next room should lead them directly down into the garage. This made him feel that they had already accomplished so much, and he now felt increasingly optimistic that Terrence was close by. "Yes, come on Debbie," agreed Larry, grabbing her hand. "Let's go pick up that brother of mine and get back to the tree."

Larry put Tinsel back down on the ground, where he

immediately began sniffing and licking Larry's injured foot. "No boy, it's okay," dismissed Larry, smiling. "But thanks just the same, lad!"

As they followed Splint towards the kitchen, Larry noticed that Tinsel was still desperately trying to get underneath his foot as he lifted it. "What are you doing? *No boy!* I know that you're just trying to help heal it, but I think it needs more than just a lick, don't you!" He patted him with gratitude. "Now go and see Splint... *See Splint!* That's a good lad."

"What was he doing?" asked Debbie, watching Tinsel run through the door towards Splint.

"I think he was just trying to help," smiled Larry, then suddenly stopped, just before the kitchen door. "Oh, hold on a minute, we almost forgot. Where are our manners!" He turned around and looked across the room to the blue light that was still silently lighting their way.

Larry tipped his hat. "Thank you kindly Mr. Blue Light, for helping us pass through your room. We wish you well." They both waved the light goodbye and walked through into the kitchen. The blue light clicked itself off and went back to sleep.

The kitchen seemed a little smaller to the travelers than the dining room, but felt so much colder as they walked across the tiled floor. The window above the wooden breakfast bench looked out into the dark night, where a blanket of thick snow lay across the back garden. Inside, a layer of frost had decorated the lower half of the window, etching winter patterns across its pane. Debbie felt a chill run through her as a cold draft passed by, carrying with it a damp, musty smell.

While walking between the legs of the breakfast bench, Splint found himself worrying about what the cat did earlier to the light. He nervously stopped walking. In front of him lay a saucer of white liquid lying on the kitchen floor. Not knowing what it was, he casually sat down on its rim, and curiously looked down at his whitened reflection in the milk. He curiously dipped his finger in the liquid, and after smelling it, carefully dabbed his tongue to taste it. He immediately cringed. "Ugh, that tastes awful...! What was I thinking?"

As the group caught up, Splint pointed to an open door at the far end of the kitchen. "It has to be over there." He rose abruptly. "Come on, let's keep moving."

"What's all that stuff in here?" asked Larry, staring down at the saucer of milk.

"Oh...! I don't know," shrugged Splint. "But it tastes terrible. My advice is stick to the sweetness of pine needles," and tapped his pine-sack.

Debbie and Larry both nodded, and stepped curiously past the saucer of milk, still unsure of its true purpose.

They all walked out from under the legs of the kitchen bench, and for the first time stayed together, quietly on alert for any signs of danger.

With the pain in Larry's foot growing ever more intense, and the constant flashbacks to the Army-Light incident with the cat playing in his mind, Larry tried distracting himself by singing softly. Once again, he found comfort in the 'Carnival Song'.

"So shake yourselves down

and stand up tall,
It's Christmas time,
So let's have a ball..."

Debbie recognized the tune and joined in, quietly clicking her fingers to the rhythm.

"So joy to you and joy to all,
Joy to you and joy to all,
But for goodness sake... Bom-Bom-Bom...
Stay well inside the Army-Light wall!
I say sta—"

They abruptly stopped singing after hearing themselves sing the words to the song and worryingly glanced at one another. Nothing was said and they continued their way quietly towards the open door at the far end of the kitchen.

They passed in front of the kitchen stove, which was about half way across the room.

"So when did you two arrive at the tree...?" asked Splint, trying to lighten the mood.

"I arrived about twelve seasons ago," answered Debbie.

"Where did you originally come from?" continued Splint.

"From a place called Sweden, where one of the children's grandma lives. She sent me over to wish the newly married couple a 'happy first Christmas' in their new house. There were only about ten of us dwellers on the tree back then. Mind you, the tree was a lot smaller then, too, for some reason, so it didn't feel that empty."

Splint glanced over to Larry. "And you, Larry?"

"Oh, it was seven seasons ago for me," began Larry. "Just after their son Aaron was born into the family, Terrence and…" He paused a moment as many fond thoughts of his brother ran through his head. "Yeah! Terrence and I were gifts from the family's Auntie and Uncle, to celebrate his first Christmas."

Larry smiled quietly for a moment, recalling waking up next to his brother on the tree that year. "And Debbie here gave us our names, didn't you Debbie!"

Debbie blushed, remembering how she fell hopelessly for Larry as soon as he opened his eyes. "I knew as soon as he slipped and fell off that branch onto me, knocking me over," giggled Debbie, "that he was something special."

Larry nodded. "And we've kept that tradition going in one shape or another every season since, haven't we!"

Debbie nodded, with a warming smile.

Splint said nothing; he just nodded as they inched ever closer to the door and the steps leading down into the garage below.

"And you, Splint?" asked Larry, returning the question. "Where did you…" They were interrupted when a loud bang and a humming sound rang from the far side of the kitchen.

"*AHH!*" They all jumped, and instinctively ran to the closest place they could find to hide, which happened to be a gap between the kitchen stove and the counter top cabinet.

Larry, closest to the gap, ran in first, writhing in pain from his foot. He was closely followed by Debbie, Tinsel and then Splint; none of them daring to look back to see what the sound was.

They all hid quietly in the dark, waiting for the sound to stop.

It did not.

Splint noticed that it was not getting any louder either, and inquisitively popped his head a little way out of the gap to see what it was. He noticed the sound was coming from a rather large white box, standing in one corner of the kitchen. It had the words 'Refrige-a-Nation' written across its top corner, and bits of notepaper and crayon drawings randomly stuck all over it.

"What is it, Splint?" whispered Larry, holding his foot off the ground, trying to keep his balance.

"I don't know, but it's not doing anything." answered Splint. "It's just standing there vibrating."

Larry took a step back to catch his balance and felt a sharp poke in his back. "*Ouch…!*"

"Shh…!" hushed Debbie, and noticed Larry was holding a small plastic ruler in his hand. It had been lying on the floor with some crayons, paper clips, an old eraser and food crumbs.

"What's all this stuff?" asked Larry.

"I've not a clue," whispered Debbie, looking more closely at the ruler.

The refrigerator turned itself off and the kitchen abruptly fell into silence. Debbie and Larry looked at Splint.

"It's stopped… Listen!" said Splint. "Come on. I think it's fallen back to sleep! It's not saying anything…" He then noticed the ruler Larry was holding. "What are you doing?" asked Splint, looking puzzled. "What's that?"

"Beats me…" shrugged Larry, dropping it back on the floor.

Splint looked back into the kitchen. He then carefully stepped out, closely followed by Debbie, Tinsel and then Larry, who was limping so badly from his injured foot that he could barely put any weight on it.

Larry only made it a few steps before he had to stop. The pain from his foot was finally too much, and he looked at Debbie, knowing what this now meant for him and his search for the box. "Debbie," whispered Larry.

Debbie looked back and noticed him shaking his head, as if to say that this was as far as he could go. "It's gotten worse?" she whispered, with concern.

Larry nodded and took a deep breath. "I think it happened when we ran into the gap just then. I felt it crack."

Debbie noticed that the crack in his foot had extended up into his ankle, and knew he must be in terrible pain. She glanced at Splint, who was getting close to the steps. "Okay... Okay..." she said, gathering her thoughts. "We'll get through this. We're all going to be fine!"

Tinsel ran back to Larry and began sniffing again at his foot. "Hey, boy! How are you doing...? Better than me, I hope?" smiled Larry, patting him on the head.

"Come on, Larry... Let's try and get you moving," suggested Debbie, trying to get him to stand on his foot. "You can use me as much as you like for support, okay!?"

"*Ouch...!*" cried Larry as his foot cracked and grated again under the pressure.

"No Larry, come on, *use* me... *Really* lean into me more."

Larry knew he was already leaning too much on her. If he put any more weight on her she would fall over too.

Suddenly Larry noticed Tinsel was trying to wedge himself

underneath his damaged foot. "What are you doing boy?" asked Larry. "I told you it needs more than a lick." Tinsel wagged his tail and began wrapping his body around Larry's foot and ankle.

"What the...?" asked Debbie with a smile.

"*Tinsel. No!*" repeated Larry.

"Hold on, Larry..." interrupted Debbie. "I think he's trying to help you ... Put a little pressure on it."

"What! You're not serious, are you?" answered Larry, looking down at Tinsel, who, wagging his tail, was now tightly wrapped around his foot. Very slowly and carefully, Larry lowered his foot to the ground and felt Tinsel flexing himself underneath, beginning to support Larry's weight.

Larry's face lit up. "You're okay down there, boy...? I'm not too heavy for you?" Tinsel pricked his ears up and again happily wagged his tail. "That a boy, Tinsel... That a boy!" laughed Larry, feeling extremely grateful.

With the aid of Tinsel and Debbie, Larry began stepping on and off his foot, checking down regularly to make sure Tinsel was still fine.

In the meantime, Splint had already arrived at the top of the stairs and was looking down into the dark garage. "How on earth are we going to get down?" he asked himself. Only a moment passed before an idea washed over his face, and he ran back in the direction of Larry and Debbie.

"Typical!" sighed Debbie under her breath as he approached.

"He finally comes over when we don't need him…"

"What is it, Splint?" called Larry with concern. "What's the matter?"

"Nothing, just hold on a minute…" gasped Splint, running past them. "We need something to get down those stairs." He ran over into the gap at the side of the stove.

Debbie and Larry stood there looking at one another, wondering what Splint was looking for.

After a short time, Splint reappeared, running back with the plastic ruler over his shoulder. "This should be fun if it works," smiled Splint, passing them again on his way back to the steps.

XIV

Down The Steps We Go

WITH TINSEL'S HELP, DEBBIE AND LARRY finally arrived at the top of the stairs. Splint had already placed the ruler out over the first step like a plank on a pirate ship, and was nervously stepping out, trying to keep his balance.

"What are you doing, Splint? You're going to hurt yourself there…" warned Larry, watching Splint bounce on the ruler.

"If this works, then my weight will swing it down, like a ramp onto the next step," explained Splint, concentrating hard. "Then you can both slide down it." The ruler lifted slowly off the kitchen floor. "Look… See!" smiled Splint.

Larry looked puzzled. "That's really kind of you Splint, but… why didn't you just tip it and slide it down onto the next step, instead of doing all this 'plank walking'…? Wouldn't that be easier, or are you a 'wanna-be pirate' or something?" teased Larry.

"Oh yeah…!" replied Splint, feeling the ruler tip further. Splint hastily tried taking a step back, but he had gone too far out and the ruler tipped even further. Larry jumped over to try and grab it, but he was too late and the ruler tipped over and slid off the edge of the step. "*AAAH!*" yelled Splint, falling backwards, desperately grabbing onto the side of the ruler. It slipped down and smacked the step below. Splint uncontrollably slid down the ruler, landing on his bottom on the step, with a thud. "*Ooh! What a rush!*" laughed Splint, checking to see that he was okay.

"You all right there, Splint?" asked Larry.

"Yeah, I'm fine!" answered Splint, patting himself down. "Come on… who wants to come down next?"

"Go on Debbie!" insisted Larry. "I'll hold the top for you up here." Debbie looked down at Splint holding the bottom of the ruler in his hands. "It's fine," urged Larry. "Now come on, let's all get down these steps."

Larry stole a quick glance back into the kitchen to make sure it was still safe, then helped Debbie climb on top of the ruler. She carefully sat down and to her surprise, immediately began sliding. "*AAAAAAH!*" she screamed, and desperately grabbed the sides of the ruler to try and slow herself down.

"You're okay, Debbie!" reassured Larry. "Now slowly ease off with your hands and you'll slide … Go on!"

"I'll try," flustered Debbie, "but it's a little bit too slippery for my liking." She carefully began releasing her fingers one-by-one. Slowly and surely she slid all the way down onto the step below, where she hastily jumped off.

"Now you, Larry!" nodded Splint, still holding the bottom of the ruler in place with his feet and holding the sides tightly with his hands, keeping everything steady.

Larry gently unraveled Tinsel from his foot and carefully sat down at the very top of the ruler, holding Tinsel tightly in his lap. "You ready, Tinsel?" smiled Larry. Tinsel wagged his tail eagerly.

"Right. I'm ready when you are Larry!" nodded Splint, bracing the ruler.

"Okay then..." answered Larry. But Larry just sat there. A moment passed.

"What's the matter, Larry?" asked Splint.

"I don't know! I'm just not moving!"

"Well, just jiggle around on it a little bit," suggested Splint. "Don't worry, I've got hold of it down here!" Larry followed Splint's suggestion.

"That's it!" said Splint. "Just jump up and down a little to get yourself going and you'll be as good as gold!" Larry jiggled a little harder, trying to get some downward motion going, but still nothing seemed to be happening. He sat there looking confused. What Larry had not noticed was that with all the jiggling, the splintered piece of his foot had dropped from his pocket onto the top step.

Splint sighed and stood up looking puzzled, taking his hands off the ruler. He could not understand why Larry was still stuck.

Meanwhile Larry had already decided to give it another go and jumped up and down as heavily as he dared, which did the trick. He started sliding down. *"Hey, I'm moving...!"*

But due to his sheer size and momentum from his excessive jumping, the bottom of the ruler popped out from under Splint's feet and slid forward out of his control. *"No, wait! Hold on, I'm not ready!"* warned Splint, lunging forward, to try to bring the ruler under control. It was no use. The ruler slid through his legs, over the edge of the lower step and down.

Splint looked up, and the last thing he noticed was a terrified Larry and a happy Tinsel sliding straight for him. They swept him up and carried him full steam ahead, past Debbie, towards the bottom of the steps.

"AAH!" yelled Splint and Larry, sliding uncontrollably over each step as if they were on a surfboard, all the way to the bottom of the stairs, where there was a loud *'snap'* from the ruler hitting the concrete floor. Splint was thrown off to the side, while Larry was somehow still sitting upright on what remained of the ruler as it spun around on the floor.

Larry was clutching onto Tinsel and still yelling with his eyes tightly shut. The spinning slowed down and the ruler finally came to a stop.

"Larry, are you okay?" called Debbie down into the darkness. Tinsel jumped out of Larry's hands and ran around excitedly, eager

for another ride.

Larry stopped yelling and popped back into his solid state from sheer fright, then rolled gently off the ruler onto the garage floor.

Splint, who without question had landed heavier out of the two, got to his feet and checked himself to make sure he was okay, then looked to Larry. "Larry… Hey, Larry! Are you all right over there?"

Larry opened his eyes with his body still in a solid state and murmured, "Are we there yet?" with his stiffened lips.

"Where…?" asked Splint, looking confused. "The box?"

"Um… Nothing..." Larry replied, sheepishly popping back into his mobile state. He got to his feet, still shaken by the ordeal. Tinsel ran over, and eagerly wrapped himself around his foot once again. "Thanks, boy…" smiled Larry, as his head slowly cleared.

"*Larry! Larry! Are you all okay down there?*" called Debbie, still squinting down from the top of the stairs.

"*Yes, we're fine! How are you up there?*" replied Larry, stepping out into Debbie's view.

She looked around on the step. "I'm fine, but I'm not sure how I'm going to get down?"

"Hold on… We'll see what we can find down here!" answered Larry, as both he and Splint set about looking for something to use.

The layout of the garage was in a rather peculiar 'L' shape and felt big and extremely cold. The large garage door was rattling in the icy wind, making the garage feel very gloomy and unnerving.

Larry shivered and looked up at a window above the garage

door, which provided the only source of light from the street. A strong wind blew in through a crack in the window.

From the top of the second step, Debbie was feeling increasingly isolated and vulnerable. Being away from Larry since both he and Splint had disappeared into the dark garage, for what felt like the longest time, had only added to her sense of unease. She peered up at the top step to see if anything was there, worried that something was staring back down at her.

"*Hey!* I've found something!" said Larry, picking up a small ball of garden string from the corner of an old wooden workbench. "This could work." He limped back to the bottom of the steps, as Splint continued to search amongst the piles of boxes and clutter.

"Hey, Debbie!" called Larry, arriving at the bottom of the steps. "Is there something up there you can tie one of the ends of this to?" and held out the ball of string.

Debbie quickly glanced around and noticed the head of a bent nail, sticking out about waist height on the front of the step. She pulled down on it, testing its strength. "Yes, I think I can use this thing," she answered, then placed her arms out in readiness.

"Ugh…!" strained Larry, throwing up one end of the string while keeping a tight hold of the other.

It rippled up through the air and although it was long enough to reach above Debbie's head, it recoiled back before she could reach it and dropped onto the step below her.

"Just a minute," said Larry. "Let's try it again!" and pulled the string back down to roll back up.

"Okay, you ready, Debbie?" asked Larry. She nodded back, and this time he threw it harder. As before, the string reached above Debbie's head, but dropped onto a lower step before she could reach it.

"No, it's not heavy enough at your end," confirmed Larry and glanced around the floor. "We need to attach something heavy to it. Hold on. I'll be back in a moment."

"Hey, Splint!" called Larry, looking eagerly around. "We need to find something to attach to the end of it!"

Splint looked up. "You need what?"

"It's too light at the moment," explained Larry. "We need to attach something to the end." Splint had a blank look on his face. "*The string!*" repeated Larry.

"Oh… Sure!" answered Splint, finally understanding what Larry was asking, and he jumped down off the boxes to help Larry.

Although they were looking in a garage full of all kinds of things, what they found was too big, too heavy or simply impossible to tie to the end of the string.

Back on the stairs, Debbie had remembered something from earlier in the kitchen and called down to them both. "Hey, guys! *Guys... Are you there…?*" There was no reply; they were both too far inside the garage to hear her.

She heard nothing, but thought that if she could get back up onto the top step, she was confident that her idea could work. She looked around for a way up, and remembered the bent nail sticking out from the step. She lifted a foot onto it, and although she could not get a firm grip with her hoof-like foot, she managed to push herself up enough for the tips of her fingers to reach the edge of the top step.

Suddenly, her foot slipped and she fell back down onto the step, scraping her arm up against the nail. "*Ouch!*" she yelped, landing with a thump. Luckily, being made of plastic, the damage wasn't too bad and with just a small scratch, she got to her feet and brushed herself off.

Looking down to the empty garage floor, Debbie decided not to waste any more time waiting for Larry, and looked back up at the top step. "Okay! This time, Debbie..." she whispered, and planted her foot firmly back on the nail. This time she managed to get not only her fingertips, but both hands over the top of the step, and with all her strength pulled herself up onto the kitchen floor.

Being alone, the kitchen looked darker and more ominous than it had earlier. Taking a final look down into the empty garage, she turned and ran towards the kitchen stove. As she neared the stove, she heard a noise from the dining room and stopped in her tracks. Staying perfectly still and quiet, she waited, listening for it again, but heard only silence. Suddenly the loud humming noise started up again from the big white box, scaring her out of her wits. She frantically dashed over and down into the gap beside the stove.

Exhausted, Debbie took a moment to catch her breath and compose herself, before she slowly and tentatively made her way further into the gap.

It got darker, the further down the gap she went. She stepped over and around the bits of crayons, elastic bands and old dried up food that littered the floor in front of her. Then she saw it. It was the paperclip, leaning up against the side of the stove. She grabbed it, swung it over her shoulder and turned back towards the opening. As she neared the gap and the open kitchen, the refrigerator stopped humming as quickly as it had begun and the room fell back into an eerie silence.

She glanced out into the kitchen for a moment to check that the coast was clear. Suddenly a noise from behind startled her and she jumped around, staring anxiously back into the darkness. A crayon had rolled off the matchbox she had just stepped over and had fallen onto the dusty floor, disappearing under the stove. Nothing else moved, but her nerves were beginning to fray.

She took a deep breath, turned around and quickly ran out into the open kitchen, back towards the garage steps. As she ran, she glanced across to the big white box, then back through the door into the dining room, where she saw the friendly blue light switch itself off. She slowed her pace, concerned as to why the light had switched itself on again. "Come on, Debbie. Pull yourself together," she whispered, and quickened her pace back to the top of the steps.

Finally arriving at the steps, Debbie could hear Larry shouting from down in the garage, "*Debbie…! Where are you?*" She felt so relieved to hear his voice.

"Where've you been?" asked Larry. "I've been worried about you! Is everything okay?"

"Yes…!" gasped Debbie, trying to get her breath back. "I got the thing we needed!" and proudly showed him the paperclip.

"That's my girl!" smiled Larry. "Now throw it down and I'll tie it!"

Debbie dropped it down and Larry turned to Splint, who was still rummaging around amongst the clutter. "*Hey, Splint!* It's okay, we've got something!" and showed him the paperclip.

Splint did not seem to be listening, and simply nodded back before continuing through the piles of clutter.

Larry went to work on tying the paperclip.

Debbie sat on the top step and twisted her body around, ready to lower herself back down. Suddenly something caught her eye from the kitchen, and she looked up, but it disappeared across the refrigerator into the dark. It happened so quickly that Debbie was not sure if it was her overactive imagination, or if there really was something out there. She looked down at Larry, still struggling to tie a secure knot, and thought of mentioning it, but left it and climbed down onto the lower step.

"This flippin' paperclip," sighed Larry, struggling with his large pudgy fingers.

"Oh come on, please, Larry…" begged Debbie. "Have you managed it?" She was wondering how long it takes to tie a knot, any knot. She glanced up above her head again, hoping the shadow in the kitchen was in fact just her imagination.

"Here you are!" called Larry, finally throwing the paperclip up to Debbie. Larry watched carefully as she hooked it over the nail and slowly began her descent down the string to the next step, then the next.

"Great stuff!" nodded Splint, noticing Debbie was making her way carefully down the steps. "Larry, make sure that when she gets down, we don't unhook the paperclip. We'll need it to get back up later."

"Sure thing..." replied Larry, watching Debbie's every move.

Splint wandered off to continue his rummaging.

It took a little while before Debbie finally made it safely to the ground, where she was met by Larry, who wrapped his arms around her.

She returned his hug and looked around for Splint. "So first of all he doesn't wait for you with your injured foot, and now he can't even wait for everyone to get down the stairs before heading off again. What is it with him...?"

Larry kissed her on the forehead and smiled. "Yeah! He's as eager as me to find Terrence, isn't he!"

"Larry," sighed Debbie, walking away into the cold garage. "What makes you so sure it's Terrence he's looking for?"

Tinsel looked up at Larry and wagged his tail, distracting him from Debbie's comment. "Oh! Hey, boy..." smiled Larry, and he watched Tinsel wrap himself carefully around his damaged foot.

XV

Those Two Bright Shadows

CREEPING FURTHER INTO THE GARAGE, they all gazed in wonder at the new and strangely shaped objects all around them. Debbie looked up towards the garage door that was still rattling in the icy wind, and followed the odd snowflake blowing in through the broken window.

None of them had the slightest notion of where to start searching for Terrence. Besides the car, there were mountains of clutter everywhere they looked, including two large workbenches covered with opened boxes and discarded tools left out to rust. To the side of the steps lay a large woodpile that had partly toppled over, spilling out across the cold concrete floor.

Splint carefully walked around a puddle next to one of the wheels of the car, and felt the tire with his hand, wondering what the huge metal box with four rubber feet was for. All of a sudden, a light appeared from behind the other side of the wheel, startling him.

Splint froze on the spot, not knowing what to do next. The light was not like the lights he knew back on the tree. This was fatter, taller and bright blue. Splint also noticed the beautiful Christmas tree pattern intricately painted on its glass body, that glowed every time the light shone.

"Guys..." Splint whispered, not taking his eyes off the light for one moment, "I think we're in trouble here."

Debbie and Larry poked their heads out from behind Splint to see what had caught his attention. The light quickly jumped back behind the wheel into hiding, seemingly startled by their appearance.

"What was that?" asked Larry.

"I thought *you'd* know," replied Splint, leaning forward around the wheel to catch where the light had gone. With care, he took a couple of steps, then another couple around the side of the wheel and disappeared out of sight.

He stepped through the dark then saw the vague silhouette of the light standing in front of him. "Hi..." said Splint. The light turned around and glowed, with the elaborately painted Christmas tree facing Splint. It flashed three or four times, paused for a moment, then jumped forward a step.

Larry and Debbie stayed on the other side of the wheel, staring at the ground around the corner, which seemed to be glowing on and off.

"What do you think is going on, Larry?" whispered Debbie.

Larry looked at her and shrugged his shoulders. "I don't know…"

The light on the ground faded, and there was silence.

Debbie cast a worried glance at Larry.

"Hey, Splint…" whispered Larry, nervously. "Hey… Are you okay around there?" There was no reply and both stood there worried from the silence.

Without warning, the garage door banged in the wind, making Debbie nearly jump out of her plastic skin.

Larry carefully limped forward, to see if he could see anything around the side of the wheel.

"Be careful, Larry," begged Debbie, swallowing hard, then she felt something gently touch the back of her shoulder. She screamed.

It was Splint, standing there with the light flashing excitedly, as though trying to say something. Debbie sighed and quickly pulled her shoulder away, giving Splint a cold stare.

"Sorry, Debbie. I didn't mean to scare you," explained Splint, turning to introduce the light. "I don't know his name but he's a bright little chap… I haven't a clue what he's saying, but he seems really friendly. Don't you, fellow!" He placed a hand on its body. "*Ouch!*" yelped Splint, yanking his hand away. "Cripes, you're hot!"

"Shame it can't tell us where they put our Christmas box," chuckled Larry, glancing around the garage. "It could be anywhere."

The light hopped over to a clear space in the garage next to the car, and flashed erratically up to the wiring around the top of the garage door. Splint, Debbie and Larry looked up to see what it was flashing at, when all of a sudden a bright yellow light lit up from within the wires and jumped out of its socket. It hopped quickly from box to box down to the ground and scurried on over to join the blue light.

They both faced Splint and flashed together like a greeting, as though they were saying hello. Splint looked at Larry and Debbie, then back at the lights. "Hi there…" replied Splint to the yellow light, which he noticed had an equally beautiful and unique Christmas tree painted on it. "So there are two of you little fellows, then…!" smiled Splint. "Where are the rest of you…?" He glanced above the garage door, where the rest of the sockets were empty of lights, and covered with cobwebs and dust. "Oh!" he acknowledged.

The lights just stood there, staring at him.

"Okay!" interrupted Debbie, trying to get back on track. "Shall we find our box."

"*Yes…!*" agreed Larry, looking around the huge garage. "Where do you think they could have put it?"

"I'll start looking over here," answered Splint, wandering off towards a pile of clutter behind the children's bicycles, closely followed by the two lights.

"Shouldn't we stay together, Splint?" suggested Larry. "We don't know *what's* lurking down here, do we!" Larry glanced around in the ever-increasing darkness. "If not, can't we at least borrow one of your friendly lights or something?"

Splint looked back at them and smiled. "Well if you can figure out how to ask one of them, by all means, they're yours."

"Um…" sighed Larry, looking completely stumped. "I see what you mean."

"Don't worry," smiled Splint reassuringly. "I'll be back in a moment, after I've checked this lot here." He paced on ahead to the boxes. "You and Debbie just stay close to one another and you'll be fine."

Larry grinned and shrugged his shoulders at Debbie, then noticed the pile of boxes stacked underneath one of the two workbenches behind them. "Come on, let's check over here while we're waiting. Looks like as good a place as any to start, hey…?" He grabbed her hand and they made their way over.

Splint arrived behind the children's bicycles and found himself amongst several boxes that were precariously stacked on top of one another. Both lights were close behind, not just following him,

but staying so close that he felt he had two bright shadows. When he stopped walking, they would stop. But unfortunately when he stepped back, they would not know what to do and he'd bump into them, which took a bit of getting used to. Splint still felt the lights were good to have around, especially when he would bend over to take a closer look at something. Then the inquisitive lights would lean out to either side and take a look for themselves, illuminating everything around them.

Debbie and Larry, on the other hand, were left in the dark to search under the workbench. Larry climbed on top of one of the boxes to see what was behind it.

"Be careful, Larry!" worried Debbie, watching him struggle over the box. She felt a bitterly cold draft blow in from the cracked window of the garage door and shivered from its intensity. "Do you see anything?"

"It's really dark, but I don't think the Christmas box is here," sighed Larry, climbing back down off the boxes. Debbie shivered again and wrapped her arms around her body, trying to fend off the cold.

Larry limped past her and over to the car in the middle of the garage. Putting his good foot in the tread of the tire, he managed to lift himself up. Standing on his tiptoes, he tried looking over the top of the workbench.

Debbie walked over and helped steady him as he struggled to keep his balance. "What do you see?" asked Debbie, her voice heavy with anticipation.

Larry noticed some small pieces of chopped wood piled on top of one another, some tools including a hammer and a saw, and a small soccer ball that was softly rolling back and forth in the wind from the window. "Nothing, just stuff…" replied Larry. "Definitely no box." He stepped down off the tire, just as Splint was returning with the two lights. "Did you find anything, Splint?" asked Larry.

"No, nothing…" replied Splint, shaking his head. "It's a big box, yeah?"

"Yes, with the words 'Christmas Box' written on it," confirmed Debbie.

"No… It's not over there. I would have definitely seen it with these two," nodding over to the lights. "So, are you both sure it's down here? Because we're going to waste a lot of time looking if it's not."

Debbie and Larry looked at one another. "Yes!" answered Debbie, anxiously looking around the garage to see where else it could be. "Well… that's what I thought I heard, anyway."

Splint's face dropped. "Hold on a minute. You *thought* you heard? *Are you kidding me?*" then glanced over at Larry.

"Yes…! Well. I may have not exactly heard him say it… *not exactly,*" stuttered Debbie. "But I thought I remembered him once say, that they tend to put the box down here in the garage."

"Who's that? Who told you?" snapped Splint.

"*I don't remember! A dweller…! Someone from the tree a few years ago!*"

"Oh…! So what you're saying is… a Tree-Dweller. A long time ago… *may… have once told you,*" laughed Splint sarcastically. "Oh that's just great. So it might not even *be* down here? I don't believe it… *all this way, for nothing!*"

"All this way!" snapped Debbie. "Look I'm sorry, but we never asked you to come, you know. And if it were up to you, you'd still be back in the hallway trying to get up the first step of the stairs, where I know for a fact the box *won't* be. So don't start criticizing me for what *I thought* I heard, okay?"

Splint turned his frustration to one of the lights. "Bet you guys knew it wasn't here, didn't you!" The lights just stood there. "You could have saved us a lot of time... if either of you could flippin' well *speak,* that is!" He sighed heavily, knowing it was not the lights' fault either.

Debbie, feeling sick with guilt and worry, looked to Larry. "I'm *so* sorry Larry. Back at the tree, I overheard you both guessing where to look first. Honestly, I really thought they put it in here… I'm sorry." She then glanced around the ominous garage.

"It's okay, Debbie," calmed Larry, trying to stay upbeat. "Looking here is as good as looking anywhere. In fact, who knows... it still could be here." Larry smiled. "We've not looked *everywhere* yet, have we…? Hey, Splint…?"

Splint had sat down on a piece of wood away from them both and was staring back at the steps that led up into the kitchen.

"Splint…?" repeated Larry, trying to catch his attention. Splint looked over, glanced casually around the garage, then shrugged his shoulders and sighed.

"Well…! Let's keep on looking, just to make sure," exclaimed Larry, and with Tinsel still around his foot, he made his way back to the workbench they just came from. Debbie followed him, fretting and hoping that she had not wasted everyone's time.

Splint just sat there shaking his head, watching Debbie and Larry struggle in the dark. Although the two lights were just standing there next to him, Splint felt them staring. "What…? *What…?*" he huffed, shifting his position.

There was an awkward pause, then his conscience got the

better of him and he got up and slowly made his way over to the workbench to help with the search.

Larry had climbed on top of one of the boxes and was attempting to look behind it in the dark.

Debbie did not acknowledge Splint as he arrived with the two lights, giving Larry the light he needed.

"Thanks, Splint!" called Larry, climbing out from behind the box.

As Larry climbed from box to box, exploring every nook and cranny, Splint would carefully shift his position so that the lights moved too, giving Larry light where he needed it.

"Hey, Larry, did you check over there?" asked Splint, pointing to some boxes further back. Debbie turned around and gave him a dirty look. Splint noticed, but tried his best to ignore her.

"Oh, didn't see those," replied Larry, carefully climbing his way over.

As Splint concentrated on giving Larry the best light to guide his way through the darkness, Debbie's attention turned to a sudden noise above them, on top of the bench. She stepped out into the garage and curiously looked up. The soccer ball was still slowly rocking backwards and forwards on the bench from the wind. She sighed with relief and looked back at Larry, who was now to the side of the bench, still climbing around the clutter. "Do you see anything?"

Larry shook his head. "No… It's not here either, I'm afraid," he said, looking out into the garage, "but we'll take another look over there." He pointed to the area Splint had checked earlier before carefully climbing down.

Debbie dropped her shoulders as a wave of despair washed over her. She felt that she had surely led them to the wrong place.

A sudden gust of wind from the window blew the soccer ball over to the edge of the workbench above Larry and Splint, where it hovered momentarily, then tipped over the edge and fell.

"*LARRY, LOOK OUT!*" yelled Debbie.

Larry noticed the danger not a moment too soon and lunged at Splint, knocking him and the two lights out of the way.

The ball bounced off the box and onto the floor, where it rolled past Debbie into a dark corner behind a wooden partition.

Splint and Larry got to their feet, along with the two lights. "Thanks for that, Larry," nodded Splint, dusting himself off. "I owe you one."

"No problem," puffed Larry, wondering where the ball had gone. He walked over to Debbie. "Are you okay?"

Debbie nodded then looked around at the partition.

"What in Pine-land was that bouncy thing?" asked Larry. "Where did it go?"

"Yes… over there behind that," answered Debbie, pointing over to the partition. They both looked at one another, realizing that they had not noticed this area of the garage before, let alone searched it.

Larry grabbed Debbie's hand and they carefully made their way over to the partition, nervous to see what was hiding around the back of it.

Once there, they paused for a moment, then carefully leaned around its corner and squinted into the darkness.

They could see very little until Splint and the two lights arrived behind them. Suddenly they noticed the outline of the soccer ball as it lay still on the garage floor. The lights slowly leaned out from behind Splint and the whole area lit up. Everyone gazed up in astonishment. There it stood, right in front of them, the huge box with the words 'Christmas Box' stamped across its brightly lit side.

XVI

The Damp Patch

HE CHRISTMAS BOX LOOKED TATTY from many years of use, and on closer inspection they could see that the word 'Our' had been scribbled on in front of 'Christmas' with a crayon, so it now read 'Our Christmas Box'.

Tinsel unraveled himself from Larry's foot and stretched out his body. "You okay, boy?" asked Larry. Tinsel replied by wagging his tail.

"Wow… we've actually found it," smiled Larry, staring at the box. The smile dropped from his face as a million thoughts scurried through his head. Debbie stepped forward, gently held his hand and smiled understandingly.

Splint, once again, wasted no time. He walked past them to look for a way into the box, closely followed now, as usual, by the two lights.

Larry took a deep breath and swallowed with nervous anticipation. Debbie glared at Splint over his eagerness to get to the box; after all, this was surely Larry's moment.

"*Hey!*" called Splint, from the far side of the box. "I think I've found a way in!" They walked around and noticed some melting snow dripping in from a small hole in the garage roof, creating a puddle next to the box, soaking one of the corners.

Splint began tugging at the wet cardboard, but it was still too stiff for him to rip.

"Hold on, Splint. Let me give you a hand," said Larry, taking a hold of the cardboard with his big gloves. Larry pulled hard and with his size and strength, it was not long before they had a big enough hole in the box to squeeze through.

As Larry stood back to make sure the hole was big enough, Splint suddenly stepped in front of him, ready to walk in. Catching himself at the last minute, Splint smiled and gestured politely for Larry to enter first.

Larry smiled back then looked at Debbie, taking a deep breath before stepping inside. "Okay... Here goes!" he said, then paused a moment, looking around. "Where's Tinsel? Tinsel, where are you, boy?"

There was a rustling sound over by the car and they all looked over. Tinsel was sniffing at the car wheel and wagging his tail, looking like he was ready to do something.

"No, Tinsel! Not there!" warned Larry. "Come here… come on boy!"

Tinsel looked up and immediately ran back over. "Come on

boy… in…" said Larry, pointing into the opening of the box. Tinsel ran inside without hesitation and Larry grabbed Debbie's hand and led her tentatively inside.

It was so dark inside the box that Larry and Debbie found it impossible to see anything at all. They stood there holding one another's hand, listening to Tinsel sniffing around.

Back outside, Splint took a last look around the garage to make sure it was safe, then walked in through the opening, followed closely once again by the two lights. As soon as the lights hopped inside behind Splint, they illuminated the whole box.

The box looked even bigger on the inside, and was littered with soft white, pink, and light blue tissues. The tissues were crumpled up in some places, but in others they looked very soft and inviting. Cardboard boxes and lids were piled up carelessly on top of one another, littering the bottom of the box around them. Nothing seemed in its place.

Splint started rustling around under tissues and pieces of cardboard, while Larry and Debbie stood there motionless, still overwhelmed by the sheer size of their bedtime home. They had never seen it this spacious, disorganized or empty of dwellers before.

Instead of following Splint, the two lights were also standing still next to Larry and Debbie, trying to adjust to the new surroundings.

"Do you know where we should to be looking?" asked Debbie, trying to get her bearings on where Terrence would have been sleeping last year.

"No... I... I haven't a clue," answered Larry, looking around the floor for something he might recognize. "It... it all looks so different like this."

Debbie glanced over at Splint rustling around under some tissue paper next to an empty box, watching him slowly lift up a large piece of cardboard.

Meanwhile, Larry limped off in a different direction, calling for his brother. "Terrence! Terrence! Are you there, bro...?" while carefully moving empty boxes and lids out of his way.

Debbie noticed Splint had suddenly stopped and was staring down at something.

"What is it, Splint?" asked Debbie, nervously walking over to him. Looking down, she was horrified to see the remains of a Tree-Dweller smashed into little pieces, and threw a hand over her mouth to stop herself from screaming.

Splint stared at her. "Is this...? Um... was that...?"

Debbie shook her head. "No, it's... It's West-Witch. I heard her sister was looking for her earlier, but I thought she'd been found, since I didn't hear anything else."

"The woman with the pointy hat and the house that falls on her every year?" asked Splint.

His question fell on deaf ears, as Debbie was now very concerned for Larry, hoping the same thing had not happened to Terrence. "Larry... *Larry!* Where are you?" shouted Debbie, leaving Splint staring down at the bits on the floor.

Larry had hobbled over to another area inside the box, far away from the brightness of the two lights. The boxes here were piled noticeably higher and Larry was more careful limping amongst them and through the tissue paper that littered the floor.

Climbing a box that was blocking his way, he slipped, falling headfirst in front of a pair of feet poking out from under some white tissue paper. Larry recognized them immediately and yelled, *"Terrence!"* anxiously jumping to his feet. *"Hey, Debbie; Splint! He's here... I've found him!"*

Larry looked back down and smiled. "Come on lazy-bones, get up!" But there was no answer. "Terrence! It's Larry... come on, get up... It's Christmas!" Larry waited again for a response. There was none.

The smile drained from Larry's face and he slowly bent over, taking hold of the tissue paper in his hand. He gently lifted it. "Terrence... is that you...?"

Not even the strongest could have prepared themselves for what Larry found hidden under the soft tissue paper. He fell to his knees, weeping uncontrollably. "Terrence... Terrence...! No! This can't be true... No...!"

Debbie heard Larry's crying and sped towards him. She joined him and, taking a glance, quickly turned away in shock and disbelief.

Larry slowly pulled away the paper from the pieces that were left of his brother and looked down at him lying there. "Why...? Why Terrence? How did this happen to you? *No...! No...!*" He started swinging backwards and forwards on his knees.

Splint finally arrived. "What's happened? What's the

matter?" He stopped abruptly when he noticed Larry kneeling by someone's side. Splint knew Larry had found his lost brother.

Looking to Larry's side, Splint was shocked to notice only the bottom half of Terrence's legs, the middle part of his body, his head and his hat, as whole parts. The rest of his scattered remains seemed unrecognizable.

Debbie knelt down next to Larry and cradled him in her arms, listening to his uncontrollable sobbing. She did not know what else to do. She could only try to make his pain a little more bearable by being there with him.

"What could have happened?" whispered Splint under his breath, and he carefully stepped around Debbie and Larry to take a closer look, taking extra care not to walk on any of the stray pieces.

Debbie heard Splint pass by and glanced up momentarily before turning back around to comfort Larry.

Splint squatted down at the other side of the body, to take a closer look at what might have happened. As he looked, a shiny piece of metal wire, poking out from underneath some glass shards, caught his eye. "What...? What's that?" he muttered to himself. He glanced back up to make sure Debbie and Larry could not see what he was about to do, then carefully nudged the piece of sharp glass away to the side and picked up the wire.

Debbie heard the glass move and looked up again to see Splint hanging over the body. She glared at him in disgust, unable to comprehend why he could not simply leave things alone and in peace.

Splint, however, was too inquisitive to notice the look and was now intrigued to see that the wire had a piece of clear glass attached to the end of it. "An Army-Light?" Splint asked himself, and looked back down at what was left of the middle part of the body. As he leaned in closer, he saw amongst the cracks a couple of strange burn-like marks that had scratched the glass. He placed the wire from his hand close to the marks to see if it matched, and it seemed to. "What the...?" Splint whispered, completely baffled by what this could mean.

He was holding up the wire in the air to get a better look in the poor light, when he noticed the glare on Debbie's face. He glanced back down at the body, and quickly realized how inappropriate it all was. "I'm so sorry," he whispered, and stood up awkwardly. He walked quickly away and out of the box, leaving them alone to grieve.

Some time had passed and Larry had cried himself to a semi-solid sleep. Debbie had made him comfortable by resting his head on some soft tissue paper, and occasionally stroked his forehead when he mumbled to himself. Larry finally calmed down and turned totally solid, falling into a deep sleep. Debbie decided to take a break and get some fresh air outside the box, after such a terrible ordeal.

Walking out, she noticed Splint sitting by himself. He appeared to be deep in thought. She wanted nothing more to do with him, and started to walk away in the opposite direction. Then she paused; she felt the need to say something. Larry may not have noticed it about him, but she felt it was about time something was said. "*Hey, you, Mr. Tactless!*" spat Debbie with contempt.

Splint looked over.

"*Yes, you!*" snapped Debbie. "Tell me then, now that it's all over… What *was* your reason for coming with us on this journey? What were you looking for in there? Because it *certainly* wasn't Terrence, that's for sure!"

"What?" replied Splint, looking awkwardly to the box, worried Larry would overhear her agitated voice. "No, I wasn't looking for anything! I was trying to help you both find his brother… which I'm really sorry about… I hope you believe—"

"*Really!*" interrupted Debbie, feeling sickened by his sentiment. "To be brutally honest, I don't believe you at all! I never have, ever since I first set eyes on you down at the bottom of our tree!"

Splint sighed and looked down, trying to change the subject. "You know I saw some strange marks on his body in there," nodding towards the box. "And whatever happened to Terrence, happened to one of those Army-Lights too. It was broken underneath hi—"

"What marks? What are you talking about now?" interrupted Debbie, not believing a word of it. "It's not strange at all. It's 'Shattered Sleeping Syndrome'!"

"What?" asked Splint.

"*Shattered… Sleeping… Syndrome…!*" sighed Debbie,

annoyed she was having to repeat herself.

Splint paused a moment. "What the heck is that…?"

Debbie rolled her eyes again, then snapped. "*I don't know!* It just happens during the long sleeps."

"All the time?"

"No! The last time was a while ago, and Tree-Lord dealt with it. It hasn't been back since!"

"I've honestly never heard of it before…"

"*Well you wouldn't have, would you!*" spat Debbie. "And stop changing the subject. What were you out here looking for…? Did you find it? I hope it was worth it!"

"I wasn't looking for anything else! Just his brother."

"Of course you were," dismissed Debbie, shaking her head. "But you're not going to tell me, are you?"

Splint stood up, ready to leave.

Debbie was still not finished. "It just seems strange to me that you'd be so interested in helping out Larry, when you don't even know him… let alone his brother!"

"Look, I… I'm really sorry about his brother. I know you don't believe me, and that's fine… But I truly am." Splint tried placing a hand on her shoulder as he walked by, but she shrugged him off in disgust.

Splint knew it was pointless to try to continue, and walked back towards the box. He looked up to the changing light outside the garage window and said calmly, "It's going to be light soon, we better stay close to the box until next dark. It's probably the safest place around here… unless that 'Syndrome' thing comes back."

Debbie said nothing and watched as he calmly walked inside

the box. She paused a moment then slowly walked back too, as the yellow and blue lights scurried out from the flap. She watched the bright lights jump quickly away over the garage floor, up the pile of boxes at the far end and back into their sockets, ready to receive a fresh charge.

Meanwhile, inside the box, Splint wanted to express how sorry he was at Larry's loss and walked slowly up to him. "Larry… um," began Splint, awkwardly clearing his throat. He was about to continue, when he noticed Larry was totally solid, in a deep sleep, then heard Debbie walk in through the entrance behind him. Not wanting to disturb Larry or confront Debbie again, Splint quickly found himself some tissue paper for bedding and disappeared to a solitary corner to settle down and get some rest.

Back outside the box, an Army-Light suddenly appeared at the top of the stairs, standing next to the piece of Larry's foot he had dropped earlier, along with a couple of chewed pine needles. The light looked down into the dark garage below, and noticed the string and paperclip hanging from the steps. It knew that the missing group was not too far away and flashed an urgent message back into the kitchen.

In the box, Splint was still trying to work out what happened to Larry's brother. He felt apprehensive about falling asleep there, but did not know a safer place to rest. At least in the box, there was less chance of them being noticed by the family.

Settling down on his tissue paper, Splint looked over at

Debbie and Tinsel, who had both cuddled up close to Larry. More of the morning light began to feed its way in through the ripped hole in the box, making Splint feel sleepy.

Back at the safety of the Christmas tree, one of the Army-Light messengers had returned with news for Tree-Lord. All the dwellers were settling back up onto their Bedtime-Branches and only the lack of a few Army-Lights around the tree seemed to show that anything was amiss.

Climbing the tree, the Army-Light passed some dwellers talking to one another about how selfish Larry and Debbie had been, putting everyone on the tree in so much danger.

Finally it arrived near the top of the tree in front of Tree-Lord, and held out the piece of Larry's foot with its electric field. Tree-Lord acknowledged it and flashed at the light, then the light proceeded to flash the latest news, but no matter how quickly it flashed, it seemed it could not get the words out fast enough.

"*What do you mean,* you still don't know their precise whereabouts!" snapped Tree-Lord. "*What have you all been doing out there?*"

The Army-Light tried flashing again to explain itself, but Tree-Lord interrupted. "*So what!* What does a shard of glass tell us!" He slapped the glass out of the Light's grip and it fell down through the branches onto the ground below. "You're supposed to find all of him, not just part of his *foot,*" continued Tree-Lord. "What good is that to the safety of the tree?"

Several dwellers looked up from their branches, wondering what had sparked Tree-Lord's outburst.

Tree-Lord noticed their concerned looks and took a deep breath before turning back to the light. He smiled and said, with a calmer voice, "Sorry, but we really do need to find them quickly, you understand. Now please, for the sake of everyone's safety on the tree, go and find them…! *Hurry!*" He flashed his orders again to the light.

The Army-Light acknowledged the orders with a series of short flashes and immediately jumped down through the branches and across the living room floor. Tree-Lord looked back at a couple of the dwellers and smiled, trying to hold in his deepening frustration. "Nothing to worry yourselves about. We'll have them all back before you know it."

Daylight filtered through the window and they all quickly fell asleep.

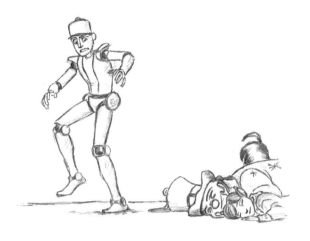

XVII

Finding A Way

SPLINT WOKE UP ABRUPTLY and glanced over at Debbie and Larry, who were still asleep. He rose quietly to his feet and softly crept over towards them. Tinsel woke up growling.

"Shh... Tinsel," whispered Splint, quietly passing them on his way over to the opening in the box.

Tinsel pricked up his ears with curiosity and watched Splint tiptoe to the opening. Splint carefully poked his head out of the box and peered into the garage, staring into the silence. At first, he neither saw nor heard anything in the darkness. Then, as he pulled his head back inside, he caught a glimpse of movement. A silhouette slid behind some boxes at the far end of the garage.

"Oh, those two lights again," muttered Splint, feeling

relieved and wondering if it was time to wake Debbie and Larry. He yawned and stretched, as the wind rattled the garage door again. He glanced up to the window and to his surprise, noticed the two garage lights were still fast asleep in their sockets. Splint hastily looked back to where he noticed the silhouette a minute earlier and wondered what he had actually seen. Pausing for a moment, not knowing if it was his sleepy mind playing tricks on him, or whether he actually did see something, he decided to play on the side of caution.

"Hey, you two…" whispered Splint, gently shaking them out of their slumber. "Come on, wake up. It's time to leave…! I'm not sure it's that safe here anymore!"

"What…?" said Debbie, looking back at Larry with concern, knowing he would not be ready to leave yet. She stood up and watched on as Splint hastily removed all traces of his makeshift bed, then quickly counted the remaining pine needles he had in his sack.

Debbie glanced back down at Larry who was now sitting up, staring vacantly at the ground. "But we can't leave. Not just yet…" she insisted.

Splint ignored her and walked over to Larry, placing a hand on his shoulder. "Look, I'm… I'm sorry, Larry. I really wish there was more time, but I don't feel it's safe for us to stay here. We need to start moving." He hastily walked away towards the opening of the box.

Debbie glared at him as he walked by. "Do you have an ounce of compassion in your whole wooden body? Well, do you?"

"Look!" whispered Splint, out of Larry's earshot. "I think I saw something out there… an Army-Light maybe, but I'm really not sure. I only got a quick glimpse."

Debbie remained quiet.

"I know it might not be anything," continued Splint, "but I don't want to take the chance. Besides, whatever happened in here with that 'Syndrome' thing or whatever you call it, I don't want it happening to me!"

"Well, if it is an Army-Light all the way out here," snapped Debbie, "that means they know we've left the tree." Her face suddenly dropped.

"What?"

"Oh no...!" gasped Debbie looking down at Larry.

"What? What is it?" repeated Splint, wondering why she was so concerned about the Army-Light. "Who cares if they know we left the tree, you need to tell them about Larry's brother." He continued walking over to the opening of the box. "And like I said, it could have been anything out there, not just an Army-Light. There're a million things out there, like that cat we saw earlier for one... though that's probably not a good example right now!"

"No, that's not it! What date is it?" asked Debbie, helping Larry to his feet and passing him his pine sack. "It's Christmas Day *night*, yes?"

"Yeah, so...?" sighed Splint, getting a little impatient with the drama.

"We all go back in the box in a little over a day!" answered Debbie.

A shocked silence filled the box.

"*What!*" yelled Splint, pacing back over. "What happened to our *'Twelve Days of Christmas'* I was told of back at the tree?"

"*Normally we do have twelve days...*" replied Debbie, "but

this year the family said they were going away just after Christmas, on the twenty-seventh. So they'll pack us all up before they leave."

"*Oh, great!*" flustered Splint, pacing back and forth.

"In fact, I think we were lucky to come out at all this year," continued Debbie. "It sounded like they weren't even going to bother getting a tree." She looked concerned over at Larry, who was still quiet and vacantly staring into space.

"Oh that's just brilliant…!" panicked Splint, wanting to head off immediately back to the tree. "Tell us now why don't you…!"

"*I'm telling you now…! Okay!*"

Splint glanced at Larry. "So come on, we'd better get going then." He swiftly made his way out into the garage.

"Hold on a minute!" said Debbie, thinking aloud to herself. "Maybe we should just stay here in the box under some paper or something like that!"

Splint reluctantly stopped. "What?"

"Well, I doubt they'll even notice we're not on the tree when they pack everyone else away. And it saves us having to make the long trip back in time."

"No Debbie, we can't…" interrupted Larry, shaking his head, talking for the first time since waking up. "How's Tree-Lord going to have time to deal with the syndrome, if we're all in the box falling asleep. Any one of us could be in danger. No, we need to get back as quickly as we can to alert him. Besides, our family on the tree needs to know what really happened to Terrence. They need to know that Tree-Dwellers don't 'just disappear' each year as everyone says… There's a reason… syndrome or not." He breathed deeply. "I owe it to Terrence."

Splint nodded. "And to the other dweller."

Larry peered at Splint, then at Debbie. "The other one...! What other one? There's someone else...?"

Debbie nodded slowly.

"Who...?"

"West-Witch," answered Debbie. "She's lying around the corner, over there."

Larry sighed and paused a moment, then slowly lifted the pine sack over his shoulder and limped towards the exit. Debbie held his hand gently, while Splint eagerly walked out ahead of them into the garage, quickly followed by Tinsel.

Even though Larry knew they urgently needed to get back to the tree, his heart was aching and his stomach sick at the thought of leaving his brother alone there. He stopped, let go of Debbie's hand and turned around.

"Larry...?" said Debbie.

"I'm fine... Go on ahead... It's all right."

Concerned, she reached out again for his hand, but Larry stepped away and smiled reassuringly to her. "Don't worry. I won't be a minute, I promise." He stepped back inside.

He slowly limped over to where Terrence was peacefully lying and knelt down next to him for the last time. He smiled at his brother's face, and slowly reached over and picked up his brother's hat. The noise of rustling paper from a corner of the box broke Larry out of the moment and he glanced away towards the sound, but saw nothing.

He looked back down at his brother again, while hopelessly trying to hold back his snowman tears. He leaned over close to his brother's face and whispered, "Bye, bro'…" then struggled to his feet and slowly limped away. Looking back, he noticed Terrence's feet poking out from under the tissue paper, before they were finally blocked from view by one of the many boxes.

Limping out of the box, Larry was immediately greeted by Tinsel, who willingly wrapped himself again around his injured foot. "Thanks, boy," acknowledged Larry, wiping away the tears. He turned to Debbie and took a deep breath, blinking heavily to clear his glazed eyes.

"Are you okay?" asked Debbie, gently rubbing his snowman arm. She then noticed Terrence's hat hanging over his shoulder.

"Yeah," sighed Larry, looking out at Splint, who having already passed the car was now hurrying towards the bottom of the steps.

"Wow, that guy can move fast!" sniffed Larry, attempting to change the subject. He chuckled. "He probably wants to get away from here before those two lights of his wake up, eh…!"

"Yes. He's definitely quick all right," sighed Debbie, knowing now wasn't the best time to bring up her deep reservations about Splint. She grabbed Larry's hand tightly and they both quickened their pace to catch up to Splint.

As Larry and Debbie arrived at the steps, they noticed Splint was already checking the tightness of the string, to make sure it was secure enough to climb back up.

"So, who's going first?" asked Splint, giving a final tug on the string. "Larry... How about you?"

Larry just stood there staring back at the ground, gently stroking his brother's hat.

Splint turned to Debbie, showing her the string. "So how about you then...?"

Debbie was unable to take her eyes away from Larry. Seeing him like this and being unsure of how to help him broke her heart.

"Debbie..." repeated Splint, trying to keep things moving. "Come on. He'll be next up... I promise."

Debbie grabbed the string reluctantly and looked up at the high steps. She glanced back at Splint and deliberately gave the string a hefty tug, checking its safety to clearly demonstrate how little she trusted him.

Debbie slowly lifted herself up the string, and was finally managing to grab onto the first step, when a loud bang suddenly echoed from the kitchen. Splint and Debbie stood perfectly still as the kitchen light switched on and the fridge door opened to the sound of rattling bottles. A moment later, and the door squeaked shut as the sound of footsteps trampled towards the top of the steps.

Panicking, Debbie's foot slipped off the step, ripping her hands from the string and she fell down on top of Splint. They both scrambled into the woodpile next to the steps while Larry, oblivious to the danger, just stood there in full view of what might come down those stairs.

"Larry!" whispered Debbie anxiously from the woodpile.

He looked round slowly.

"*Come over here!*" she begged. "*They'll see you…!*"

He walked lethargically towards them until Splint jumped out and grabbed him by his sweater, pulling him down into the woodpile.

"You're right!" called Dad from the kitchen. "The draft was coming in from the garage! One of the kids must have left it open again!"

Splint poked his head out from behind the woodpile just as Dad slammed the kitchen door shut. The light under the door disappeared, along with all hope of them getting back up into the kitchen.

In complete shock, Splint slumped down behind the woodpile and the sound of footsteps finally disappeared. "*NO!*" cried Splint. "*No! I don't flippin' believe this…! UGH…!*"

"What is it? What's wrong" asked Debbie, staring at him for an answer.

"I knew we should have left earlier!" snapped Splint, and he abruptly stormed off into the garage. "How the heck are we going to get back to the tree?" he blurted, pacing backwards and forwards through a small puddle. "We're totally cut off!"

"*What…!* You're kidding!" gasped Debbie, jumping from the woodpile and looking up the steps.

"I'm not!" confirmed Splint.

"*No…!*" panicked Debbie, staring at the closed door. "We're not going to make it back, are we! I don't believe this!" She slumped to the ground, holding her head in her hands. "What should we do now?"

"It beats me," admitted Splint, kicking the water from the puddle.

"Larry, what do you think?" asked Debbie, looking through her shaking fingers.

With a vacant look, Larry simply shook his head and mumbled, "Whatever you think, love..." then stared back at his brother's hat.

Tinsel unraveled himself from Larry's foot and wandered away.

"*Hey, Tinsel!* Come here boy...!" yelled Debbie, calling him back, but Tinsel ignored her and disappeared amongst the darkened clutter.

Debbie got to her feet and desperately tried thinking of a way out of the predicament. She looked around, hoping something would come to her, but feeling cold, anxious and emotionally exhausted, she found her mind completely void of ideas.

At times like these Debbie usually turned to Larry for help, but being totally beside himself with grief, she knew he was in no shape to help anyone right now. The frustration and hopelessness of the situation was all too much and she broke down into tears.

Splint finally stopped kicking the water from the puddle and calmed himself down. He overheard Debbie sobbing and was unsure of what to do about it, besides looking for another way out. He immediately started looking around.

He carefully stepped along the sides of the garage walls, feeling for any holes they could crawl through, which would lead back into the house, whether it was to the kitchen or any other room.

Unfortunately, without the help of the friendly lights from

yesterday, Splint found himself stumbling over the clutter, until he tripped and landed heavily on the floor, banging his elbow. *"Ouch! That's it. I've had enough...!"* he griped and stormed out into the open area of the garage. He looked up at the two lights above the garage door and yelled, *"Hey...! Hey, you there! You guys! Wake up...!"* But there was no sign of life from the lights – they remained dark, sleeping peacefully in their sockets.

Splint quickly proceeded to climb the boxes next to the garage door, in hope of actually shaking the two lights awake. He swiftly clambered to the top and jumped up at the wires they were sleeping in, but it was hanging up too far out of reach. *"Hey, you two...!"* called Splint. *"Psst...! Wake up...!"* But there was no response. "Are you kidding me, lights? *I don't believe this! It's typical... just typical!"* Frustrated, he looked down into the garage, wondering what to do next.

"What are you doing up there?" asked Debbie, drying her face.

"What? What does it look like I'm doing! I'm trying to wake them up! We're never going to find a way out of this *blasted place* without lights! I can't see a flippin' thing down there!" He glanced back at the lights, hoping to see a flicker.

Debbie sighed. "You're wasting your time…"

"What...? How do you know?" sighed Splint.

"They probably didn't get switched on today."

Splint stared at her, confused. "Switched on...! What do you mean…?"

"For the— *Ugh!"* moaned Debbie. "They need to be switched on to charge themselves up, so they'll stay asleep until they've been switched on again…! You'll be shouting well into tomorrow before they'll help you again."

Splint groaned at the sleeping lights, knowing it had been pointless. He again scanned around the garage from high up on the boxes, but it was too dark to see anything of importance, so he climbed back down.

Once down, he was making his way back towards Larry and Debbie when he heard Tinsel barking close by. Splint hurried over. *"What is it, Tinsel…?"*

Out of the darkness Splint found Tinsel barking and wagging his tail at a squeaking cat flap blowing in the wind. Splint noticed the flap led outside. He could see snowflakes falling at the other side.

"Good boy!" smiled Splint, and called over to Larry and Debbie. *"Hey, you guys…! Tinsel's found something! Come quickly!"*

Debbie grabbed Larry's hand and smiled. "Come on, Larry! Tinsel's found something!" and helped him to his feet.

Walking slowly over to Splint, Debbie noticed just how badly Larry was limping with his injured foot.

They arrived just as Splint was struggling to slide an empty nail box underneath the cat flap.

"Hey, Larry…!" said Splint. "Can you give me a hand over here?"

Without a word or a nod, Larry limped over to help push the box.

"Okay, after three," nodded Splint eagerly. "One… Two… and Three…! *Ugh!*" The box slid against the wall beneath the flap. Splint smiled and slapped Larry on the arm. "My, you're not half built like a brick pr—" He stopped as he caught the vacant look on

Larry's face. He turned away knowingly and focused on getting them all out of there as quickly as possible.

Splint noticed the box was high and he would still need help climbing on top of it. "Sorry, Larry… excuse me…" called Splint. *"Larry…!"*

Larry finally looked up.

"Could you please help to push me up?"

Larry silently limped over and cupped his hands together.

"Thanks," acknowledged Splint, and placing a foot in his hands, lifted himself onto the box. He immediately walked out of sight.

"So, what do you see?" asked Debbie.

There was no reply, which worried Debbie, and she glanced across at Larry and grabbed his hand.

Larry smiled, still looking at the ground, completely oblivious to what was going on around him.

Debbie took a step back trying to look over the top of the box. *"Splint… What are you doing up there? What's the hold up…?"* She could still neither see him nor hear him, which unsettled her nerves. She suspected he had already left the cat flap and had stranded them there. "Has he gone…?" she huffed. *"Splint…!"*

"Yes…?" replied Splint, reappearing at the top of the box with a couple of snowflakes on his face. "What was gone?"

"Nothing. I didn't say anything," answered Debbie.

"Okay then," shrugged Splint, holding out a hand. "Come on, we can get out and I think there's a way back in at the other side of it, too!"

Debbie hastily picked up Tinsel and passed him to Splint,

who was surprised to receive an affectionate lick on the cheek from him, before putting him down on top of the box.

Debbie paused a moment. "Hold on a minute. 'The other side' of what…?"

"Of what…?" replied Splint, wiping his cheek dry.

"*Yes! Of what?*" huffed Debbie impatiently. "You said you 'think there's a way back in at the other side'! The other side of *what?*"

"Of out there!" answered Splint. "Across the other side of all that white stuff, there's another opening that's flapping in the wind. It must be a way back into another part of the house." He offered a hand to help her up.

Not exactly sure of what to do, but knowing there was no other way out of the garage, Debbie reluctantly grabbed his hand and he helped her up. Once safely on top of the box she snatched her hand back.

In return, Splint made an obvious attempt to wipe his hand clean on his leg. He then stepped over to the edge of the box to help Larry. "Okay, come on Larry!" nodded Splint, holding out his hand.

Larry was still caressing his brother's hat and staring blankly at the ground.

Debbie clicked her fingers to try and attract his attention. "Hey, Larry, come on…!"

Larry slowly looked up, slid his brother's hat carefully over his shoulder, raised his hands and grabbed onto Splint and Debbie.

"*Pull…!*" shouted Splint, and they pulled with all their might. Larry was large even by snowman standards and quite heavy, but putting their differences aside for a moment, Splint and Debbie worked together and finally managed to pull Larry safely up onto the top of the box.

They all walked over to the clear plastic cat flap that was blowing in from the icy wind. Tinsel had already stuck his head out through the flap into the falling snow, wagging his tail in eager anticipation of what lay ahead.

XVIII

A Very Yellow Landing

THEY ALL KNELT DOWN AND CAREFULLY looked out under the flap. This was the first time any of them had experienced snowflakes, now gently falling onto their faces and into their inviting hands. One thing they could all agree on was how icy cold the wind felt as it blew against them.

Splint looked out through the snow to determine how far it was to get back into the house, while Tinsel barked and attempted to eat each and every snowflake that passed in front of his nose.

"I think that's the entrance back into the house, over there…" explained Splint, pointing to another flap at the far side of the snow covered garden.

Debbie squinted through the snow over to where he was pointing, then looked down and noticed just how high up they were.

"So how do we intend to get down…?"

Splint looked down and realized there was nothing to climb down with, just a huge drop between them and the ground.

There was a moment's silence as snowflakes continued to fall.

"I know!" said Splint, snapping his fingers. "I'll go back and try unhooking that paperclip and string from the steps!" He tried standing up. Just then, Tinsel stretched a little too far grabbing a snowflake and slipped out off the ledge.

"*No!*" yelled Larry.

Tinsel fell yelping from the great height down into the deep snow, where there was a *'crunch!'* then silence. Everyone looked down onto the snowy ground, expecting the worst.

Suddenly, the snowy lump below them shifted around and Tinsel jumped out wagging his tail.

"Tinsel boy…. *You're fine…!*" smiled Larry in relief, watching Tinsel shake the clumps of snow off his back, then barked back up at them.

"Wow... It's really deep! The white stuff cushioned his fall!" smiled Splint. Tinsel jumped up and down and rolled around in the snow, loving every minute of this new experience.

Splint eagerly stood up on the outside of the flap and looked around, making absolutely certain there was no other way of getting down.

"What are you doing?" asked Debbie.

Suddenly Splint slipped on a piece of ice and fell over the edge. He swung out a hand and grabbed onto the ledge.

Larry lunged forward and grabbed his other hand, while

Debbie hesitated a moment, until her conscience took over and she too jumped forward, to help.

Splint could feel his fingers slipping from the ledge. "I'm losing it!" he strained, and his hand quickly slipped off, causing his whole body to twist violently, pulling his other hand from Larry's grip. He fell down into the snow with a loud '*crunch*', disappearing beneath it.

Larry and Debbie stared down into the snow looking for signs of movement.

Suddenly Splint's hand popped up out of the snow, giving a 'thumbs-up' sign. He quickly climbed out, shaking the snow off himself. "Wow…! Now *that* was a rush!"

"Are you okay? You're not hurt?" asked Larry.

"No, I'm fine. It felt soft, like it caught me..." He looked down at his imprint in the snow. "And look how deep I went... That was great! Now come on, you two! What are you both waiting for? It's easy, isn't it, Tinsel!"

Tinsel barked back in agreement.

Debbie glanced at Larry as he grabbed hold of her hand. "Ready then…?" she asked, swallowing hard.

"Yes... We need to get back to the tree," answered Larry, knowing that this was the only way out of the garage.

They carefully stood out on the ledge, watching Splint checking the snow below them. "*Hey, Larry!*" called Splint. "I think you can fall about here if you can! It's really fresh and soft…!"

Larry nodded.

"And, Debbie," continued Splint, looking up through the falling snow. "You'll need to land a little ways away from one another! We don't want you falling on top of each other, now, do we!" He smiled, then pointed to what looked like another deep snowdrift. "So right about here looks good, okay!"

"You trust him?" murmured Debbie, from the side of her mouth.

"What do you mean?" asked Larry, looking puzzled by the comment. "Where did that come from…?"

"Well, we don't really know him, do we…?" suggested Debbie, feeling a little awkward.

"Come on," said Larry, dismissing her question. "Let's get down and back to the tree."

Checking to see that he was standing exactly over where Splint told him to, Larry gently let go of her hand, took a deep breath, leaned slowly forward and closed his eyes. "One, two, three…" He fell.

Debbie watched him fall, and land with a dull 'thud!' He disappeared beneath the thick white blanket.

Splint ran over and peered down into the big hole Larry had made in the snow. "You all right down there Larry…? Everything okay?"

Debbie was too afraid to ask anything and just waited anxiously on the ledge. Suddenly, she noticed a red gloved hand push up through the snow and Larry's head appeared.

"Yeah, I think so," answered Larry, and was helped out of the snow by Splint.

Debbie took a deep breath, knowing it was her turn now. She checked her position again to make sure it was above the spot Splint had pointed out, then closed her eyes and slowly leaned forward into the snowy air. She felt herself falling and screamed.

The scream ended abruptly with Debbie landing with a *'flop!'* in the snow. Larry and Splint both scurried over and she sat up out of the snow.

"Fun, huh?!" asked Splint, leaning towards her.

Looking a little dazed, Debbie took a good look around, then down at the snow she was sitting in. "What's all this…?" she asked. "The snow…! It's… It's all yellow…!"

Larry immediately looked over at Tinsel, who was away digging around in the deep snow.

Tinsel stopped playing and looked back at him, and barked excitedly.

"Oh, no! Don't tell me…!" huffed Debbie. *"NO! THAT'S GROSS…!"* She glanced an evil eye at Splint as Larry helped her up.

Splint calmly pointed at the deeper snow to the left of her, which was brilliantly white, thus putting the blame back on her for falling in the wrong place. He nodded to Larry before walking out through the snow towards the other cat flap.

Debbie huffed in frustration while she attempted to brush the less-than-white snow off herself, before a stain could set in.

Having quickly walked a good distance in the deep snow, Splint looked back to Debbie and Larry and noticed they had not yet started walking. *"Come on, you lot…! We have to get there before we all freeze to solid…! It's too cold to just be standing around!"*

Debbie was already shivering badly and she noticed Larry had dropped back into his despondent mood after helping her out of the snow. She gently placed a hand under his arm. "Come on, Larry! He's right, we're going to freeze out here if we don't get moving."

Splint watched them trudge slowly through the snow towards him, when from the corner of his eye he noticed a large mountain of snow at the far end of the garden, near the shed. He squinted, then smiled, pointing it out to everyone. *"Hey, Larry...! Now that's a bit strange wouldn't you say...! Looks a bit like you, doesn't it!"*

They had stumbled upon a huge snowman that Aaron and Emma had made, with their parent's help, on the afternoon of Christmas Eve. It had ended up so big and tall, that both Mom and Dad had to help lift its heavy head up onto the top of it. It had a big hat just like Larry's and an umbrella over its shoulder. Plus it had a long carrot for a nose and big pebbles for eyes, mouth and the buttons down its front.

"Wow...! It really does!" said Debbie. "My, that's *amazing!* It's like a huge copy of you Larry...! *Larry, over there!"*

But Larry was not looking. He just gently nodded and continued walking.

Splint took a final glance at the giant snowman before turning around to continue carving a path through the deep snow.

Splint noticed that with each new step, his feet sank further into the snow, making it that much harder to walk.

Losing his breath, Splint stopped and looked around for an easier way, and noticed the snow at the side of the house did not look as deep; possibly being a little more sheltered from the swirling wind. *"Hey, Larry, Debbie. Let's move closer to the house...!"* yelled Splint, pointing towards the house. *"Looks like it could be easier to walk through the white stuff over there, okay!"* He changed his direction towards the house.

Tinsel stopped playing when he heard Splint yelling through the snow and quickly jumped across the snow to Larry. Shaking the snowy clumps from his coat, he wrapped himself around Larry's foot, ready to help him this time through the snow.

Tinsel did not seem at all affected by the cold. It was as though his thick and bushy strands of tinsel were keeping him extra warm and insulated.

"Good b... boy Tinsel," acknowledged Debbie, shivering badly in the biting wind.

Splint arrived at the side of the house and found he was right about the snow not being as deep there, making it a little easier to walk through. He continued setting the pace towards the far end of the garden, a pace that Debbie and Larry found impossible to match. They both fell further behind.

"S... Sp... Splint...!" shivered Debbie, calling as loud as she could through the snow.

Splint abruptly stopped, but did not turn around.

"F... For goodness s... sake!" continued Debbie. "Just wait, would you...!"

Splint looked around with an intense frown on his face.

"Shh...!" He seemed to be listening for something.

"W... What is it?" stuttered Debbie, looked anxiously around the garden.

It was difficult to see anything clearly through the heavy snow and near darkness. Only the shape of garden objects lying underneath the deep blanket of snow, could be seen.

Along with the cold, a worrying feeling sent a shudder through Debbie. With the phrase 'safety in numbers' running around in her head, she felt an urgent need to get the group back together, and quickly.

Splint was still listening for something as Debbie and Larry caught up.

"Wha'...? What is it...?" asked Debbie, shivering far worse than either Larry or Splint.

"Shh..." replied Splint, placing a finger over his lips. "Did you both hear that...?"

Freezing in the wind, Debbie listened as best she could, but the cold had finally taken its toll on her. "I don't feel very good... My legs...! I'm... I'm just... just going to lie down for a minute. Just for a minute," when her legs buckled and she fell against Larry.

Larry caught her fall and tried keeping her moving on her feet, worried that she would turn solid and be unable to wake up. "Debbie, Debbie! Come on. Stay with us, now...!"

"Just sleep for a minute, I promise!" mumbled Debbie.

"No, you can't!" insisted Larry, shaking her awake.

Splint felt inside his pine sack and pulled out his last two pine needles. "Here, have her take these! They might help."

Larry quickly placed one of the frozen needles to her lips.

"Come on, chew on it, Debbie... That's it," and watched her slowly chew on some well-needed nourishment.

Ahead of them, the cat flap squeaked in the wind. "It's the cat flap," murmured Debbie, as her head began to clear. "For goodness sake, Splint! It's the flap that you heard!"

"No, it wasn't coming from over there," answered Splint. "It was something else," and blinked up into the night air, as large wet snowflakes fell against his face. He continued listening.

Staring at Splint, Debbie suddenly realized that she had not seen him shiver once while being outside in all the snow. "Why aren't you cold?" she asked.

"What?" said Splint.

"And why are you making us slow down?" continued Debbie suspiciously. "One minute you can't wait to get back to the tree, and the next you're holding us up out here in the freezing cold, listening to nothing. You sure you want us all to get back to the tree?"

"*What...!* Of course I do!" defended Splint, looking confused. "I'm solid wood, which I guess might—"

"Whatever, Splint," interrupted Debbie, waving his reason away with her hand. "I don't care what you say any more. You can do what you like, but just know this... *We're* not going to freeze out here, you got that...?" She grabbed Larry's arm. "We're getting back to *our tree...!*"

Splint watched them struggle past him through the freshly fallen snow, then he glanced back out into the dark garden and said quietly, "But I'm sure I heard something..."

After a moment's pause, Splint turned and hurried over to catch up with the group.

XIX

Under The Blanket

HE PEACEFUL SILENCE OF EARLY MORNING surrounded the cold dwellers, as they pushed on through the snow towards the cat flap.

Debbie desperately needed to get herself and Larry out of the cold as quickly as possible. Larry was still quiet and subdued, while Splint, for the first time since leaving the tree, was at the back of the group, deliberately keeping himself a few steps back from Debbie. He was still listening for that sound.

"Ouch…" mumbled Debbie, feeling a sharp pain running through her left leg. She glanced at Larry and without him noticing, carefully looked down and felt the outside of her leg. She noticed the seal which joined both halves of the leg was beginning to split apart when she bent her knee; a result of the intense cold. Not wanting to concern Larry with more than he was already struggling with, she kept on walking through the snow, trying to ignore the pain, knowing it would naturally heal itself if they could make it out of the cold.

Suddenly a loud '*crack...!*' echoed around them all and they stopped.

"What was that?" asked Debbie, looking worryingly out over the snowy garden.

"That was it! That's what I heard!" exclaimed Splint, hurrying in front of Debbie and Larry. "I told you I heard something!"

They listened again, but only the light patter of snowflakes landing gently on the ground disturbed the silence.

"Come on!" said Debbie. "We're so close to the opening! Let's get there quickly!" She gently helped Larry along, passing by Splint.

Splint stayed where he was and slowly looked up at the rooftop. Blinking heavily through the falling snow, he noticed what looked like a small flash of light, like a spark; followed by a loud '*Crack...!*' that echoed loudly above their heads.

"*WATCH OUT!*" yelled Splint, and he lunged forward towards Debbie and Larry, but it was too late. A huge pile of snow fell down upon them, burying them all in a dark and eerie silence.

Larry opened his eyes and tried to focus, but all he saw was blackness. He tried moving his body, but was stuck fast. As panic set in, he heard a sniffing sound close by above his head. "*Tinsel...!*

Tinsel! Is that you…?" he gasped, and heard the sniffing getting louder. He felt his hand being grabbed and pulled up through the snow. It was Splint.

"Larry, you all right?" strained an exhausted Splint.

Larry finally popped out above the snow. "Thanks, Splint. Yeah, I'm fine…! And you?"

"Yeah, though I don't know what—"

"Where's Debbie?" interrupted Larry, glancing over the huge piles of fallen snow for any sign of her. "Where is she?"

"I don't know... You're the first one we found, and that's all due to Tinsel. I didn't know *where* to look. I was shouting both your names, but I couldn't hear either of you."

"*DEBBIE!*" yelled Larry, stumbling over each bolder of snow. "*DEBBIE, WHERE ARE YOU?*" He started digging frantically into the thick snow wherever his feet landed.

Splint did not know what to do or where to search either. The roof avalanche had covered a truly massive area, compared to the size of the small Tree-Dwellers.

Tinsel, wagging his tail, ran over to Larry and began digging with him, as though it was a game.

"Tinsel, boy! Go find Debbie…" sniffed Larry, as tears trembled down his face. "Find my Debbie… f… find my Debbie." He gently pushed Tinsel away, as he hopelessly broke down crying in the snow.

Splint watched Tinsel scramble away over the snow. It was obvious to Splint how much Debbie and Larry meant to one another. For Larry to lose her too, and so quickly after his brother, would surely be too much for him to bear, let alone anyone else.

No one knew which bolder of snow she could be buried under. All Larry and Splint knew was that time was quickly running out for them both, as she would soon freeze to death down there.

Tinsel began barking and digging in the snow, a short distance from where they both stood. He stopped for a moment and sniffed at the snow. Then, confirming the scent, he carried on digging.

Larry jumped to his feet and ran over. *"DEBBIE!"* he called, and slipped clumsily in the snow, falling into Tinsel's hole.

Splint ran over too and they desperately dug into the bitterly cold snow. *"I'm here, Debbie! I'm here!"* yelled Larry. *"Hold on...! Just hold on...! I'm coming!"* He hoped she could hear him.

Larry noticed something beneath his hand in the snow and gently pulled it out. It was one of the pigtail ribbons from Debbie's hair. Hopeful, he shoved his hands into the same spot, digging faster and faster. "She has to be here...! She just has to!" he sniveled. He felt his hand touch something other than snow and pulled away. It was a hand, a cold hand. Splint stood up and stepped back.

Larry leaned in and grabbed the hand firmly. He took a deep breath and with all his might, pulled as hard as a snowman could. Slowly and surely Debbie appeared up through the snow.

"Debbie!" blurted Larry, kneeling down. "Debbie, what have I done to you...?" He gently cradled her cold, stiff body in his arms. "It's all my fault. You should have never come out with me..." He rocked her backwards and forwards with tears streaming uncontrollably down his face. "Come on, Debbie! Don't leave me... Please don't leave... Not now...!"

He looked down at her pale face and gently wiped the clumps

of snow from it. He stroked the small antler above her left ear, something she always loved him doing. "Stay with me! Stay with me! Oh, come on, please... Come back to me!"

Splint stood there looking at them both, not sure what else he could do. A few moments passed and the wind finally began to drop, allowing the snow to fall gently.

Larry closed his eyes, cradling Debbie tightly in his arms, not wanting to let go.

He felt a hand gently grab his shoulder, and opened his eyes expecting it to be Splint. But Splint was standing in front of him, a few steps away.

"Larry...?" coughed a weak voice in his ear. "What happened...? Ohhh... I'm so cold..."

He watched Debbie slowly start popping out of her solid state, limb by limb.

"You're okay...!" blurted Larry, with fresh tears running down his cheeks.

Debbie coughed again.

"Don't you ever leave me again... *You hear me!*" continued Larry, as though he was telling her off for giving him such a fright.

"I won't..." she coughed, still trying to clear her throat. "Are we there yet...?"

"Hey, you!" laughed Larry. "That's my line...!" He held her ever closer. "I don't ever want to lose you, and I'm sorry I've been away in my own world since leaving the garage."

Debbie interrupted him, gently stroking the side of his face. "No... no... Shh... You had every reason to be... I totally understand."

"But—"

"Shh..."

Larry gently nodded and looked at her. "But let me promise you something here and now; that from this moment forward, I'll always be there for you. *Always!*"

They kissed and Larry gently helped her to her feet.

Tinsel, faithful as always, jumped over and wrapped himself around Larry's foot.

"Oh, yes, how's your foot doing, Larry...?" asked Debbie, still shivering slightly.

"It's doing fine, thanks to Tinsel. Hey, boy!" he said, and looked down at him. "And he's the one that found you, too! Don't think we'd still be here without you, boy." Larry patted him on the head with a big smile.

Splint, keeping his distance, smiled quietly to himself, then turned and slowly led the way once again towards the cat flap.

He now purposely walked a little slower than he had previously, making sure everyone was keeping up with him. He would also look up occasionally to check for any more snow that could slide off the rooftop.

The snow began to lighten as they finally arrived at the opening.

Splint noticed the flap was low enough to the ground for them to climb into without the need for boxes. Wiping the frost from the flap, he looked down into the tube-like tunnel. "Okay! There seems to be a room at the other end," he confirmed. "Let's climb in!"

They lifted up the heavy flap and carefully climbed under it, into the shiny metal tube. The warmth of the house immediately washed over them and they all sighed with a welcome relief.

They tiptoed down to the end of the echoing tube and carefully looked out into the room. Although the room appeared to be filled with a huge array of strange boxes and none of them knew where the room would actually lead to, they all felt much better than they had outside.

Splint jumped down out of the tube first. "It looks like a bedroom full of boxes."

Larry looked for a bed, but could not seem to find one. "What sort of bedroom doesn't have a bed, and is just filled with boxes…?" He lowered himself out of the tube and turned around to help Debbie down.

Splint shrugged. "Maybe they just store stuff here… I don't know." He looked around at all the clutter. "Wow! They like to hold onto stuff, don't they? Why, look at it all!" Splint then started looking for a way around the boxes, to get out of the room.

Larry noticed Splint had gotten his second wind and seemed ready to carry on. "Hey, Splint! Would you mind it if we stayed here to sleep? We're both totally exhausted, we've still got tomorrow to get back, and it's going to be getting light in a short while, too!"

Splint tried his best not to show his disappointment, but Debbie could tell he was tormented by Larry's suggestion. It confirmed her suspicions that Splint must have his own reasons for wanting to get back to the tree.

"But look!" insisted Splint, pointing out through the cat flap.

"There's still so much night left! Can't we just..." He noticed the look on Debbie's face.

"Look, Splint. *We're all* desperate to get back to the tree. But in case you didn't notice," said Debbie, forcefully pointing out through the cat flap, "we nearly didn't make it *back in* from out there!"

"It's okay, Debbie..." interrupted Larry, trying to calm things down.

"*No, Larry! I'm sorry, but I'm sick of him!*" replied Debbie, finally needing to say what she had been thinking for some time now. "He doesn't care about any of us! He doesn't care about your foot, about me, *or* what happened to your brother. He couldn't care less about anyone except himself!" She turned back to Splint, who just stood there staring at her. "*We're* staying here to rest! So unless you want to carry on alone, which is just fine by me, I suggest we *all* get some rest until next dark!"

Splint, appearing unruffled by the comments, quietly turned to walk away.

"Right, then!" coughed Debbie, still suffering from the effects of what happened earlier in the snow. "That's it! Go on without us! You'll be better off just having yourself to worry about! You know, why change the habit of a lifetime!"

"Hey, hey... I think you've said enough now, don't you?" interrupted Larry, wondering what had come over her. "Let's just leave it there and go and get some sleep." Debbie sighed, noticing the concerned look on Larry's face.

"I'm sorry, Larry. It's just him."

"Yeah, I know you're upset," said Larry, understandingly,

"but ease up, okay! We've *all* been through a lot."

Debbie turned and slowly walked towards the corner of the cluttered room and felt her split leg beginning to heal from the new warmth. Larry glanced back at Splint, who had been searching for a small piece of cardboard to sleep on. "Hey, Splint," whispered Larry. "Sorry about that. I really don't know where that came from."

Splint nodded in acknowledgment and dragged the piece of cardboard away with him, towards a corner, near a table leg. Larry watched him settling down on his cardboard bed, before turning away to catch up with Debbie.

XX

Really A Basket Case?

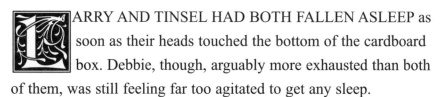

ARRY AND TINSEL HAD BOTH FALLEN ASLEEP as soon as their heads touched the bottom of the cardboard box. Debbie, though, arguably more exhausted than both of them, was still feeling far too agitated to get any sleep.

It was still not quite light yet and Debbie decided to get some air. She carefully lifted Larry's arm from around her and quietly slipped away. Leaving the box, she looked back and noticed Tinsel had woken and was quietly watching her. "Shh…! Stay boy…!" whispered Debbie.

Sighing heavily, Tinsel dropped his head and fell quickly back to sleep.

Walking out into the open, Debbie noticed Splint sitting down on a matchbox facing away from her. He was staring down the tube of the cat flap, watching the early light of the day slowly rise. He heard her footsteps but did not turn around.

"Hey!" said Splint, holding up the pine needle he had been sucking on. "I took this from Larry's sack over there. I hope he wouldn't mind, I didn't have any left."

"Well, you'll have to ask him that!" dismissed Debbie, then stood quietly for a moment. "I'm surprised to see you're still here… After all you don't need us, and we're just holding you up from getting back to the tree. Or wherever it is you need to get to!"

Splint sighed. "Yes… of course, the tree."

Debbie stared at the back of his head for a moment, wondering what he was thinking. "So why do you seem even more eager than us about getting back to the tree? It doesn't make sense? What is it you're after there? Did you leave something...? Because you definitely didn't leave any family or friends!"

Splint said nothing and continued sucking on his pine needle, to Debbie's frustration.

"Okay…! So, if you can't answer that, Splint, just answer me this one question and I'll leave you alone... What didn't you find in our box that you were after?"

Splint stopped sucking on the needle.

Debbie noticed and quickly added, "After all, that's why you came with us to the box, isn't it! There was something there you were after. You couldn't care less what happened to Larry's brother…!"

"It's not what you think!" answered Splint.

"Oh, and what *do I think*, Mr. Know-It-All! You tell me! Cuz to be honest, I *really* haven't a clue!"

Splint sighed again. "Family…"

"*Family!*" snapped Debbie, amazed at how uncreative his answer was. "What...? What would *you* know about family!" She assumed his comment was an attempt to gain some kind of sympathy. "So, go on then, about your family... let's hear it!" invited Debbie, interested in what elaborate lie he would come up with.

Splint took a deep breath and placed both hands over his face. It had never been his intention to tell anyone what his reasons were for helping Larry, but knowing Debbie's mistrust of him, all he could do now was to tell her the truth and hope she would believe him.

He turned to Debbie and paused a moment, thinking of where to start. Then, taking a deep breath and rubbing his hands nervously on his wooden trousers, he began.

"I had a brother... in fact, I had two. We were all fresh and new, out of the box, and proudly sat hanging from the small Christmas tree in a shop. We would watch the whole world go by from those branches. We were on there for a very long time."

Debbie quietly listened, enjoying how imaginative he had become with his storytelling.

"Then one night," continued Splint, "I simply woke up and found myself alone at the bottom of a basket... a 'Bargain Basket', to be exact; a basket for the *'one-offs'* that no one seemed to want." He paused a moment, hearing Larry mumbling to himself in his sleep. Larry quickly settled down and Debbie found herself listening more intently, as Splint continued with his story.

"So, that's all I know about them. There was no one else around me to ask where they had gone, so I didn't know what to think. I obviously tried climbing out of the basket at night to look for them, but I was too small and the sides of the basket were just too steep and slippery. I ended up just sitting there alone night after night, sometimes noticing things that had come and gone during the day from the basket, but not me. Well, not until the day Mrs. Ferguson found me and brought me back here to the house. So when I woke up on the tree, and heard about Larry, I, um… I thought that if I helped him find where *his brother* went, then maybe I would find where *my brothers* went, too." Splint paused, and glanced up at Debbie hoping she was still listening; she was.

"I hope you know I didn't mean any disrespect to Larry or his brother… or to you either." nodded Splint, rubbing his hands nervously together. "I'm not like that… I'm sorry you got that impression and I'm so sorry about his brother, I truly am. So anyway, that's why I wanted to get back to the tree so quickly."

"I don't understand."

"To ask Tree-Lord if he knows where they could have gone, before everyone gets packed away again back in the box, for *another year*. Which would mean *another year* of me not knowing a thing about my brothers."

"But why didn't you mention this earlier?" questioned Debbie, shaking her head. "We would have understood!"

"Because it was *my business*. Besides, I didn't know anyone back there, so why should they care about *my* problems, when they obviously cared so little for Larry's!"

Debbie thought for a moment, then nodded quietly, feeling guilty for judging him so wrongly. She did not expect to believe the story, but for some reason she did. He was not the selfish guy she had made him out to be; he was simply alone, trying to find where he came from and where he belonged.

"Um… well…!" stammered Debbie, noticing the light of the day starting to crawl into the room. "We'd best get some sleep if we're going to get back to the tree in time." She slowly turned to go back to bed.

Splint looked back out at the nearing dawn and nodded in agreement.

Debbie stopped at the small box and looked back. "Hey, Splint…"

He looked over.

"I'm sorry about earlier," said Debbie, and quietly walked inside.

Splint sat there by himself for a bit longer, sucking on the pine needle and reflecting on the whole series of events, before finally retiring too, to get some well-needed rest.

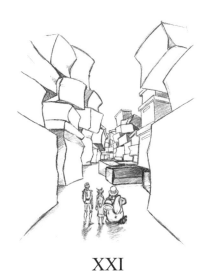

XXI

Amongst The Boxes

THE LIGHT OF DAY HAD PASSED, and darkness had once again crept over the small group. Larry awoke and noticed that it was time to move on. He nudged Debbie gently, and smiled as she opened her eyes.

"Come on Debbie, time to get moving," whispered Larry.

She reached up and grabbed his arm before he could go and wake Splint. "Hold on, Larry, it's about Splint."

"What is it?"

Debbie quickly repeated the story Splint had told her during the night; about him losing his own brothers, and how he hoped that helping Larry find Terrence, might somehow lead him to find his own.

"I didn't know what to say after he told me," admitted

Debbie. "I feel terrible for saying all those awful things to him out there in the snow. I really thought he wanted to leave us out there."

"Now, why would he give you his last two pine needles if he wanted to do that."

"He did! When was that?"

"When you were about to freeze into solid, before we got buried under the piles of snow. Don't you remember?"

"I remember chewing some, but I didn't know who's they were... I was pretty out of it."

"Yes, you were," nodded Larry, softly stroking one of her antlers. "Anyway, come on. Let's wake him and get back to the tree, so we can try and sort some of this out."

Tinsel, as always, dutifully wrapped himself around Larry's injured foot, before Larry limped outside the small box over to Splint. He grabbed Splint by the shoulders and shook him awake. "Come on, lazy-bones! Let's get back to the tree before we miss getting packed up."

Splint glanced around the room and noticed it was dark, then saw Debbie appear from the box looking ready to leave. He quickly jumped to his feet and checked to see that he had everything with him, then followed them out into the piles of boxes, towards an open door at the far end of the room.

Splint was still feeling tired from walking through the snow, more so than he cared to admit, and found himself yawning loudly as he followed Larry and Debbie.

They approached a darker area of the room and were about to walk around a particularly tall box, when Splint, while yawning again, took a quick look back at the cat flap. He noticed a shadow pass across the far end of the room, close to where they had been sleeping. He blinked several times to help clear the sleep from his eyes, and to confirm what he saw, but it had again disappeared.

"Hey, you guys!" whispered Splint, feeling the need to share his concern. "I just... well, I think I just saw a..."

"A what?" replied Debbie, glancing only partly around.

Splint hesitated a moment. "Um... a light, I think," muttered Splint quietly to himself.

"Come on, Splint!" exclaimed Debbie. "Wow, I never thought I'd be the one telling *you* to keep up!" She smiled. "Come on, or we're going to lose you!"

Splint was still unsure of what he saw back there and, not wanting to worry anyone further, decided to keep it to himself. He did, however, now link it to the time outside in the snow, when he thought he saw a flash of light on the roof. And again earlier in the garage, when he mistook a shadow for one of the overly friendly lights.

Splint hurried forward and once again led the group. Even though Tinsel was softening Larry's step, it was still causing him great pain. With Splint being slightly smaller and far more agile, it naturally made sense for him to lead the group, to check around each and every corner.

They found themselves standing in the middle of the darkened room, with boxes piled high all around. A light was still visible at the far end from the open door, but with so many piles of boxes blocking their way, it started to feel more like a huge maze than anything else.

"So, which way do we go now?" asked Splint, knowing they

had to either take a left or a right around a very large box. "Shall we split up?"

"Are you kidding? No way!" exclaimed Debbie. "We got here together; we're going to stick together! Isn't that right, Larry?"

Larry was holding his brother's hat and was chuckling quietly to himself.

"Larry...?" asked Debbie, glad to see him smiling, but curious to know why.

Larry paused a moment. "Oh, sorry... yeah, I'm fine!" The room brought back memories of when Larry and his brother used to play games, chasing one another around the wrapped presents at the bottom of the Christmas tree.

"Okay then, let's try the left..." decided Splint, and led them around that corner.

Immediately, they ran into another box, then another and another. With every turn through the thickening maze of boxes, the light from the door seemed to get dimmer and dimmer, and as the boxes got bigger and more confining, the room grew darker and darker.

"Are we sure this is the right way out?" asked Larry cautiously from the back of the group. No one answered and he stopped and looked back. "It's getting a bit too dark, don't you think...? How about we turn around and go back to the first big box, then start over? Did anyone keep track of our turns? Anyone...?"

No one answered. "Guys... hey, guys, I was saying...?" Larry looked back around.

Debbie and Splint had disappeared.

"Hey, you two...! Where are you...?" smiled Larry, looking

around the next box, thinking they were playing games with him. "Okay then…! Coming, ready or not!" He poked his head around the next one, only to find himself in front of another, even bigger box.

"*This isn't funny, you know!*" yelled Larry, just standing there. He waited a moment, but there was no answer.

"Oh, great!" he huffed. "This is just terrific." and looked down at Tinsel. "Did *you* see where they went? Left or right…?"

Tinsel pricked up his ears and just stared back. "Yeah, that's what I thought, Tinsel… Thanks boy…" sighed Larry. "Okay, then! Let's go left again." They turned left.

As soon as he did, he heard a sound from around the other side of the box that caught his attention. "Hey, Debbie, is that you?" he whispered, and heard the sound again. "Hey, come on, it's not funny! Stop messing around, you two!"

He hurried around the corner, expecting to see Debbie, but found himself standing face-to-face with an Army-Light, glowing and pulsating at him.

"Oh… It's you…!" sighed Larry, thinking the game was over and he would be escorted back to the tree. "Do you know the way out of here? You see, I'm totally lost and we really need to get back to tell Tree-Lord the syndrome's back!"

The light just stood there.

Larry continued. "Did you happen to see Debbie and Splint by any chan—"

Without warning, the Army-Light jumped up at him with its two wires jutting out in front, seemingly trying to stab him.

"*What are you doing!*" freaked Larry, deflecting the light away from his face with an arm, only to knock it down across his stomach.

"*Aaghh!*" screamed Larry in pain, and confused as to why the light would lunge at him. He glanced down at the burn mark through his creamy white sweater. "Hey! What do you think you're doing…? *It's me, Larry!*" He looked back and noticed the light was still glowing erratically. "*You could have killed me there!*"

The light hopped back, then lunged forward, attacking him again.

"*NO!*" screamed Larry, dropping to the ground, trying to cover himself.

Suddenly there was a huge flash and a shower of sparks, and bits of glass rained down around him. Larry slowly unclenched himself and looked up. It was Splint, who was standing over the light, holding a rusty nail tightly in his hand.

Larry looked back at the broken light next to him on the floor and saw it blink, then dim and go out.

"What happened? *Are you okay?*" called Debbie, running over.

Larry was stunned. "The thing just lunged out at me, as though it didn't know who I was! It was mad, flashing and everything! It just *attacked* me for no reason!"

"I know you two don't want to hear this," said Splint, still gasping from the adrenaline rush, "but I think a couple of them have been following us for a while."

"Following us?" asked Debbie with concern. "*All this way…!* So they know we've left the tree, then!" She looked at Larry. "But why would they leave the tree to follow us?"

"Maybe to bring us back?" shrugged Larry.

Debbie was confused. "But it doesn't make any sense! Why would that one want to hurt you?"

No one had an answer.

Splint helped Larry to his feet. "What's that? Are you okay, Larry?" asked Splint, noticing Larry was holding his stomach.

"I'm okay. It's where the light caught me," replied Larry.

Splint took a closer look.

"Now that's interesting…" said Splint, looking strangely puzzled.

Larry looked worried, afraid his wound was worse than it felt. "What is it…? Am I okay…?"

"Yes, don't worry, you're fine," answered Splint, and paused a moment. "It's just that your mark looks exactly like the ones your brother had."

"What are you saying?" questioned Larry. "You think it wasn't the syndrome? That it was an Army-Light that did *that* to my brother…? *Are you crazy?* Why would it want to do something like that?"

"I don't know," answered Splint, "but it looks like one's just tried to do the same thing to you. So you'd better start thinking, and fast."

They all looked down at the broken light on the floor before Splint asked the obvious question.

"Could they have something against you or your brother?"

Larry shrugged his shoulders. "The lights? Why, no! Everyone loved my brother. I think, didn't they, Debbie? Even the two children couldn't stop fiddling around with him, which at times 'drove him up-the-tree' it did!"

"Well there must be something wrong with some of these lights then. They're not taking orders and they're freaking out or something," suggested Splint, poking the dead light with the rusty nail.

"So, let's get back and see Tree-Lord before someone else gets hurt," nodded Larry.

"Right, then," agreed Splint. "We need to keep moving as quickly and quietly as we can. If there's one around here, there could be more." He looked at Larry. "Are you okay walking a little faster?"

Larry carefully felt the burn mark on his stomach. "Yeah, I think so."

"No Larry, I think he means your foot…" corrected Debbie. "Is your foot holding up?"

"Oh yeah, that… I'm fine, thanks. Tinsel's doing a great job, aren't you boy!" Tinsel wagged his tail and wound himself a little tighter around Larry's foot.

Splint felt the weight of the nail in his hand and hastily slid it into his belt. "Somehow, I think it might be a good idea to hold onto this." He looked around, checking to see that the coast was clear. "Come on! We should keep moving and this time, let's *keep together*."

They crept off into the dark forest of boxes, towards the distant light of the door.

"So where did you both get to?" whispered Larry.

"Just about here," replied Splint, "then we noticed you'd wandered off."

"I wandered off! Hey, now… It was you two who disappeared, not me!" defended Larry. "I stayed where I was. I just turned around and you'd both gone. I couldn't believe it."

"Whatever!" smiled Debbie jokingly, as they entered the densest and darkest area of the room.

They carefully walked through the canyons of boxes that piled high above their heads.

It was not long before they all started wondering if their minds were playing tricks on them, or if they really were hearing strange scurrying, scratching sounds, fading in and out of the silence.

Larry, still shaken by what had happened earlier, noticed lights flickering along the edges of boxes high above their heads.

"Hey, you two!" whispered Larry, sounding concerned. "I know I'm probably freaking out here, with what happened earlier and all, but do you see—"

"Yeah, I know, Larry," whispered Splint. "I see them too. Keep moving! We're getting close to the door!"

Strange sounds began emerging from all sides and the odd crackling spark projected strange looking shadows against the sides of the boxes. Tinsel was growling and Larry pulled Debbie in close, ready to protect her.

The strange sounds abruptly stopped and they felt an eerie silence fill the room.

Suddenly a dozen lights jumped down from the boxes above their heads, attacking them with their electrifying wires, trying to burn them.

Debbie screamed as Larry deflected a blow pointed right at her. "*AAAAGH!*" he yelled, as an Army-Light clipped his arm, shoving him into a large box.

Bouncing back up, Larry immediately grabbed his almost empty pine sack, and swung it around to deflect another light from hitting Debbie.

The light smashed in mid air and sparkled into a thousand pieces.

Larry spun around just as a wild hit caught him on the back of the neck and he fell to the ground.

"*LAAARRRRY!*" screamed Debbie, seeing him collapse into a heap.

Meanwhile, Splint was using his nail like a sword, frantically swinging and stabbing at the vicious lights, all the while yelling at the top of his voice. Sparks flew everywhere in the mayhem as his nail connected with the attackers.

"*RUUUUN!*" yelled Splint, as a light hit Debbie's arm and she was flung helplessly to the floor.

Larry scrambled over and helped Debbie to her feet, then instinctively swung around his brother's hat, swiping another attacking light out of the air.

As Larry and Debbie stumbled for the door, Larry noticed a loose nail in front of him between the floorboards and grabbed it. He looked back. *"Come on, Splint!"* and saw him being viciously attacked from all sides. "Hold on, Debbie!" yelled Larry. "He needs us!" and turned back to help.

"NO, LARRY!" screamed Splint. *"Get back to the tree and warn the others! GOOOOO!"*

Larry hesitated a moment as a light struck him on the shoulder. Unseen in the chaos, the strike had severed the string on his brother's hat and it fell away behind Larry, onto the floor. Larry quickly recovered from the glancing attack and in a moment of true hatred, swung his nail around at the light, hitting it full on. It was flung into the side of a box, where its wires punctured through the cardboard, getting itself stuck.

Larry ran back to Debbie and through the confusion and fear they stumbled for their lives towards the door, while Tinsel clung desperately to Larry's foot.

Larry again glanced back to see if the lights were following them, but they had all focused on Splint. He was still yelling at them to escape, when he finally disappeared inside the swarm of sparking lights.

Running frantically through the open door, Larry and Debbie found themselves back in the main living room of the house. The fire was still glowing, and life over at the tree looked to be as peaceful and tranquil as ever.

XXII

His True Colors

ARRY AND DEBBIE RAN SCREAMING towards the tree as fast as they could. *"HELP! HELP! You're all in danger! It's the lights… the lights! We're being attacked by some of the lights!"*

The perimeter of Army-Lights around the bottom of the tree opened up, and the Dwellers up on the tree stopped what they were doing and looked out to see who was shouting.

The dwellers on the tree gasped when they noticed it was Larry and Debbie.

"Everyone! Everyone! Now, please listen!" begged Larry, trying to catch his breath. "We've just been attacked by some of the Army-Lights! My brother was killed by one in the box while we were all sleeping!" He pointed back to the door they came in from. "And

Splint's still *out there* fighting them off! We *have* to go back and help him!"

There was total silence from the tree.

"*Tree-Lord!*" yelled Larry. "*There's something wrong with some of your lights! You need to stop them!*" Again there was only silence from the top of the tree.

Larry and Debbie looked up at everyone. They merely stood there, staring back.

Debbie shouted with frustration, "*Don't you get it...? Are you all deaf or something? We really need help, he's dying out there!*"

Larry grabbed her shoulder.

She noticed the shocked expression on his face. "*What?* What is it Larry?"

"Where are the rest of the Army-Lights, Tree-Lord?" called Larry. Once again, he got no reply. "*Tree-Lord! Where's your army gone?*"

A soft voice from the tree interrupted. "Tree-Lord sent them out to bring you all back safely."

Larry started to question everything. "You needed *that many* to go and find us?" and swung the nail out towards the door they ran in from. "And you call *that, safely...?* I don't believe it. Those are our lights out there, aren't they Tree-Lord? Why are they attacking us?"

An Army-Light hopped a little closer to Debbie and Larry jumped between them, lifting the nail up, ready to swing it like a baseball bat.

"Back off, light...! Tell it to back off, Tree-Lord! I mean it! I'm not afraid to use this!" warned Larry, readjusting his grip on the nail. "I don't trust any of them right now and none of you should, either!"

A current of shock ran around the tree. No one had ever seen a dweller act so aggressively before. They all lived such a peaceful and happy existence; to see Larry act in such a way towards an Army-Light was shocking, to say the least. To some, it was unforgivable.

"Oh, come on everyone, please!" begged Debbie. "Why are you all just standing around gawking! We're really telling you the truth! There are some bad lights out there and we have to help Splint... Now please come on, he's still out there!"

"Splint... Who's that again?" asked a voice from the tree.

"Who would want to kill your brother?" called another. "And you say you saw him?"

"*Yes!*" shouted Larry, begging for someone to believe them. "We went back to the box... we saw him there... well, what was left of him. *It was awful!* We thought the 'Shattered Sleeping Syndrome' was back again, but now I'm thinking he was actually murdered by one of *them!*" He pointed at the light with his nail.

"Why would our lights murder your brother?" asked another voice on the tree.

"*Yeah!*" yelled another. "And why do you expect us to believe you? That story's crazy! Where's the proof?"

"Well, there was a broken light lying next to him!" replied Larry, noticing some dwellers already shaking their heads.

"Okay, then look! If you don't believe me here's his hat!" said Larry, quickly patting his body. "Oh no, it's gone!" He glanced back at the room, and realized he must have dropped it in the scuffle. "His hat... I... I did have his hat, I promise you."

"Yeah, sure," laughed a voice in the tree.

Larry turned back to the tree almost in tears, before he

remembered. "And about the lights attacking me, well look at this... we have the marks to prove it!" and lifted his jumper.

At the same moment the Army-Light hopped closer to Debbie, scaring her.

Larry's reactions were quick and decisive, and he swung the nail around as hard as he could, hitting the light full on, flicking it into the air.

Debbie crouched down screaming, as sparks cascaded down over her.

"*I TOLD YOU BEFORE...!*" yelled Larry, already swinging the nail back the other way. He smacked a leg of the light into the other, causing it to short circuit and drop to the floor like a stone. It twitched and spun around in circles a few times, buzzing like a dying fly before its body finally stopped. With a twitch, its light went out.

Screams and gasps cascaded through the tree, as the shocked dwellers struggled to come to terms with what they had witnessed, an out of control Larry had just murdered one of their own.

The lights around the bottom immediately stood to attention and jumped towards Larry.

Larry looked up at everyone on the tree and realized how his actions must have looked.

"But look!" pleaded Larry, lifting his sweater again to reveal the burn marks. "This is what one of your lights — I mean *our* lights, did to me earlier!"

"*PREPOSTEROUS!*" shouted Tree-Lord, after keeping quiet all this time. "I've had enough of this nonsense!" He angrily flashed a signal down to the lights on the ground. "*Grab them both!*"

The lights quickly surrounded Larry and Debbie. Their electric fields emanated from their exposed wires, and they held Larry and Debbie firmly by their arms and legs.

Tinsel yelped from the electric shock and dropped from around Larry's foot, scurrying off behind the tree.

Larry lost his grip on the nail and it dropped to the ground with a clatter.

"Attacked... *You?*" snapped Tree-Lord. "One of our very own Army-Lights?" He glanced around at the shocked faces on the tree. "Who's ever heard of an Army-Light attacking one of us? Anyone...?"

A few dwellers shook their heads, as Tree-Lord turned back to Larry with a look of disgust. "That's so, so shameful!" tutted Tree-Lord. "And you say your brother was *killed by one too?*" His sarcastic laugh echoed around the room. "Complete and utter poppycock!"

"But Tree-Lord, please listen to me! There's something wrong with some of the lights...!" Larry insisted, struggling against the lights' containment field. "You need to believe me, for everyone's sake here! *They're dangerous!*"

"I really don't know what happened to you two while you were out there, and to be quite frank... I don't really care anymore," said Tree-Lord, and he pointed down to the dead light lying beside Larry. "These lights were sent out to bring you home *safely*, and all you can do to thank them, is attack one, like some... *crazed maniac!*"

Tree-Lord took a moment to glance around again at his dwellers, who were now transfixed on every word he said. "So if *anyone here* has the eyes and actions of a murderer, it has to be you Larry, does it not, my—"

"*NO! You* sent them out!" interrupted Debbie, struggling with the lights' electric field. "So you tell us! Why *did they attack?*"

"*THEY DIDN'T! And don't ever interrupt me again, girl!*" spat Tree-Lord, infuriated by her interruption.

"But you're—"

"*That's it! Shut her up!*" ordered Tree-Lord, clicking his fingers to the lights.

The six lights holding Debbie immediately intensified their electric strength. She screamed in agony before passing out.

"*Debbie!*" shouted Larry, and snarled back at Tree-Lord. "You better not have hurt her, or I'll—"

"Or you'll what?" interrupted Tree-Lord, calmly raising a brow. "Kill *me*, like you did our light?"

Larry held back from saying anything.

Tree-Lord continued in a stern voice. "You two are in *so* much trouble, I don't know *where* to begin!" He flashed down to the lights holding them both. "Now bring them up here!"

Larry tried resisting but it was useless. The lights' electric field lifted him off the ground along with Debbie and quickly carried them over to the tree and up onto the lower branches. Tinsel ran out from

behind the tree and followed Larry and Debbie.

"But look everyone!" begged Larry, as they passed by dwellers on the lower branches. "What we've said is all true! You have to believe us! We're all in danger!"

The dwellers simply moved well out of their way.

Larry continued struggling against the lights' grip. "Can't any of you see, something's not right here? Darrel, Sydney, come on! Why can't you all see it…? At least help Splint, he needs you out there! *Someone, please…!*"

The dwellers were overcome by fear and confusion, and just stood there staring at the spectacle. It was as though Larry and Debbie were two strangers.

Larry overheard a couple of the dwellers mumbling to one another as he passed by. "Who's that Splint guy he's talking about?"

"I don't know, I've never heard of him before..."

"Yeah…! He's playing us like fools! It must be a trap! He just wants us all to go away from the safety of the tree and *'bam!'*, we'll get the same treatment the light just did!"

Larry heard more of the same comments as they were carelessly dragged further up through the tree. He passed by dwellers he knew and loved, shaking their heads at him in disgust, while others simply turned away altogether to avoid eye contact.

One dweller, though, stared long and hard at Larry with contempt before angrily blurting out, "How could you have risked putting us all into so much danger by going out there? Everyone on the tree is our family. How could you have been *so selfish*?"

Larry did not have a reply for him; he was simply too shocked and confused at how he and Debbie were being treated, and what they were being accused of.

Larry passed by Little-Cone who stepped out from behind the safety of his mother and worryingly tugged on her apron. Her hand quickly came down and gently guided him back behind her.

Larry smiled and softly whispered, "It's okay, Little-Cone. Don't worry... you and your brother just stay close to your mother now, and you'll be fine."

Larry's frustration turned into despondency, as he continued to see the family he loved so dearly, glare at him with total contempt. Not only had he lost his brother and nearly Debbie, but now he had also lost the love and respect of his tree family, who could only see him now as a cold-blooded murderer.

Looking back out at the door they both came running in from, Larry finally realized it was now far too late for anyone to go back and save Splint. The lights would have surely finished him off by now.

As Larry and Debbie were being dragged through the last few branches on the upper part of the tree, Tree-Lord began to address his dwellers, speaking as though he was reading from a parchment.

"They understand the actions of murdering one of our own!

They know what they did by breaking the perimeter of the tree!

There are penalties for those who deliberately oppose the Elder's wishes!

Those laws were handed down to protect us all!

Those who oppose those laws, oppose our values and put us all at risk!

As a consequence, they TOO shall now be broken, as they did our laws...!"

Sounds of shock and horror echoed around the branches below, as Tree-Lord sealed the fate of Larry and Debbie.

Larry again tried to struggle free of the electric fields that were dragging him, and briefly managed to get a hand free, but two other lights jumped in and were able to bring him back under control.

Finally, Larry and Debbie were delivered to Tree-Lord.

"Tree-Lord, I beg of you! *Please…!* Just think for a moment," began Larry, looking intensely frustrated. "Can't you tell there's something wrong with some of the lights?"

Tree-Lord looked out into the room for a moment as though he was considering the thought.

"*We really did get attacked,*" continued Larry, hoping Tree-Lord would reconsider his story. "And we wouldn't have gotten back here to warn everyone if it weren't for Splint. He kept them at bay so we could get away! Please, you have to get help out to him!"

"Hmm… Splint…" thought Tree-Lord for a moment. "I've never heard of him! Obviously another one of your lies. We here on the tree are not stupid, you know!"

A voice suddenly popped up from the branches below. "Oh yeah, Splint! We know him, Tree-Lord, don't we Max? He's a good chap, he is…!" It was Dan, who was glancing around the branches looking for Max to support his comment. "Hey, Max, where did ya go?"

"Shh…!" whispered Max, hiding behind a thick branch, trying his best to keep out of the situation.

Dan shrugged and looked back up to see Tree-Lord glaring down at him. Everyone on the tree knew Tree-Lord hated nothing more than being interrupted, and that included Dan, who smiled nervously back at him, then jumped away out of sight.

"*Dan...! Max...! Come back out!*" begged Larry, as Tree-Lord slowly turned back to address him.

"As I said," continued Tree-Lord. "*I've* personally never heard of a *'Splint'* living here on the tree!" .

"*But he does...!*" moaned Larry, trying again to break free of the lights. "You can't do this! *You just can't!*"

"Oh, I can..." whispered Tree-Lord, leaning forward very calmly. "And I will, you know!"

Larry glanced at Debbie, who was still unconscious. "At least let Debbie go! She had nothing to do with it. I made her show me where the garage was! *Please let her go!* She hasn't harmed anyone!"

"She knowingly broke the laws as you did!" insisted Tree-Lord. "You've both given me no other option!"

"*Just talk to the other lights...!*" begged Larry a final time.

Tree-Lord's expression changed momentarily, just long enough for Larry to notice.

"What is it..? You know this is wrong, don't you, Tree-Lord! I can tell you know something's not right here!"

Tree-Lord leaned forward in his socket and whispered very calmly and quietly in Larry's ear, "I don't know a thing..." and pulled away with a satisfied look on his face, too subtle and too high up for any of the other dwellers to notice.

Larry's face dropped. "What's that supposed to mean...?"

"Absolutely nothing..." replied Tree-Lord, smugly shrugging his shoulders.

Suddenly from below them, a voice shouted, *"Hey, look everyone! Look, out there...!"*

XXIII

Much More Than A Twinkle

HE TREE-DWELLERS LOOKED OUT across the room, and saw Splint standing just inside the same doorway Larry and Debbie entered from, still holding the nail in his hand.

He fell into the room and the Tree-Dwellers gasped in amazement. They watched with open mouths as Splint, utterly exhausted, climbed back to his feet and stumbled forward, trying to make it over to the tree.

"Hey, that's him! *It's Splint!*" exclaimed Larry. "He's still alive! *I told you he's real! That-a-boy Splint!*"

Tree-Lord looked shocked and somewhat ruffled, watching this character stumbling out into the room.

Then, without warning, an Army-Light appeared from behind

the door.

Tree-Lord flashed desperately across the room to the light, then yelled at the top of his voice, *"NOOO...! DON'T...!"* knowing what the light was about to do in sight of everyone on the tree.

It was too late. The tired Army-Light lunged at Splint, viciously attacking him from behind. The Army-Light sparked then immediately exploded, releasing its last ounce of energy into Splint's battered body.

Splint dropped to the floor in a ragged heap and Terrence's hat slid from his hand out onto the floor for everyone to see.

"It's his hat... It's Terrence's hat!" yelled a voice from the tree, and other voices joined in.

"Was he telling the truth...?"

"Why did the light just... *Tree-Lord!"*

Shock and confusion began to spread through the Tree-Dwellers.

Tree-Lord, meanwhile, knew he needed to say something quickly to bring things back under control, but struggled to find an explanation for the light's attack on Splint. Lost for words, he just sat there looking flustered.

Splint, with very little energy left in his fragile body, managed to stumble back to his feet.

"Help him! *Please, someone!"* begged Larry, struggling relentlessly to get out of the lights' grip.

"*You shut up!*" spat Tree-Lord, losing his composure. "Mister flippin' goody-goody… I had had *enough of that* from your brother. I mean, how popular can a fat snowman get?"

"*What?*" said Larry.

"He's just a snowman, for crying out loud!" snarled Tree-Lord.

Meanwhile the Tree-Dwellers were noticing the Army-Lights beginning to pulsate brightly along with Tree-Lord.

"*What...!* What do you mean?" demanded Larry. "What are you talking about, Tree-Lord?"

"*Exactly!* You haven't a clue have you…! *None of you have!*" replied Tree-Lord angrily, as he turned to address everyone on the tree. "You're all just as *pathetic* as one another! Naive little pine eaters, going around in your own little world...! Let me explain something to you all. I'm the one that protects *all of you*. I have *all the power!*" He raised both arms in the air as his glass body pulsated ever more brightly. "But what sort of appreciation do I get from them out there…? *None!* They just throw me onto the tree any which way, then spend all their time pampering and having fun with *all of you lot…!*"

The tree was filled with terrified faces as Tree-Lord glared back at Larry. "Just imagine how it feels to be like this… Constantly stuck in this wire… *Year in, year out and every single time being totally overlooked!*"

"What…?" gasped Larry, as everyone stared in shock and disbelief at Tree-Lord's confession. Everyone had noticed the Army-Lights glowing in sync with Tree-Lord, pulsating with ever increasing anger.

Tree-Lord continued. "Yes! Every... single... year! Stuck in that blasted box! Wanting and waiting! Then when it's time, I just watch all of you enjoy yourselves with the children, *'helping make Christmas time all glittery and magical...!'* Makes me sick, it does! Especially that insipid brother of yours, Terrence! They couldn't put him down last year. You all remember? *'Ooh! What a lovely little Snowman...!'* Blah... blah... blah...!"

"W... What...?" stuttered Larry from his dry mouth, completely dumbfounded by the confession. "You mean, *you* killed Terrence? *You* killed my brother...?"

"I didn't *exactly* do it..." sneered Tree-Lord, looking smug. "But if I remember correctly, at the time I was surprised no one else woke up with all the commotion in that cramped box. It took them so much longer to finish him off than any other. I thought we'd *never* get rid of him. You know... Like one of those bad smells!"

Larry lashed out at the lights, trying to break free of them, but it was all in vain; he could only glare back at Tree-Lord with repulsion. "You were so worried about us finding this out in the box, weren't you?" said Larry, with angry tears in his eyes. "So you sent your lights out there to do your dirty work; to make sure that whatever secret you were keeping would be kept safe."

"We're coming, Splint, we're coming!" called voices from the tree, as a second Army-Light appeared from the door behind a tired and weary Splint and quickly scurried towards him.

Larry glanced out across the room and noticed the light. *"SPLINT, LOOK OUT!"* he warned. *"BEHIND YOU!"*

The light sprung up high in the air and was ready to finish Splint off, when suddenly out of nowhere appeared the house cat. It pounced over and swept the light into the air with its huge claws, smashing it into little pieces, causing sparkling lights to shower down behind Splint.

Splint continued dragging himself relentlessly towards the tree, seemingly unaware of what had just happened behind him.

He was still a good way from the tree's relative safety, when the cat turned its attention to him.

Realizing the threat from the cat, the perimeter of lights around the bottom of the tree scrambled back up into the branches towards their sockets.

The frightened dwellers just stood there, helplessly watching from the tree and trying their best to keep out of the way of the Army-Lights, who were scurrying back to their sockets to glow ever stronger with Tree-Lord.

"Splint, lie down...! Just lie still!" screamed Larry. But Splint was oblivious to the warning and carried on struggling forward.

"Now everyone shut up, and don't dare move!" demanded Tree-Lord. "Unless, of course, you want to know what a *'light shock'* feels like!"

Tree-Lord now had the whole of the tree held captive by the lights, and looking down into the room, began reveling in anticipation of the upcoming show between Splint and the house cat. "Oh what a show this will be... this *should* be good!"

Everyone looked on helplessly at Splint's plight, as the cat crouched down behind Splint and eyed him with extreme interest.

The cat's tail swung wildly from side to side, while it patiently watched Splint stagger forward towards the tree,

completely oblivious to the danger lurking behind him.

Without warning, the cat sprang up and with a razor sharp claw, flicked Splint into the air like a puppet. It batted at him again as he tumbled through the air. Then, briefly losing interest, the cat allowed him to fall to the ground, a little closer to the tree.

The dwellers gasped in shock. Some of them could not bear to see what was happening and covered their eyes.

Splint remained motionless on the floor, his eyes closed, beginning to feel numb with the pain. He slowly opened one of them and turned his head to see how close he was to the tree.

The Tree-Dwellers concerns quickly switched from Tree-Lord and the Army-Lights to the cat, as it casually swaggered over towards Splint and closer to all of them on the tree.

"Stop moving, everyone! You're going to bring the cat over," whispered Tree-Lord. "Stop moving, darn it!" He backed up his warning by having his Army-Lights glow brightly.

Splint quickly scrambled to his feet and ran towards the tree again, using every ounce of strength left in his little body.

The cat quickly leapt forward and whipped Splint back into the air, his limbs spinning like those of a rag doll. It then flipped him several times and finally finished by flinging him over into the lower branches of the tree.

The dwellers screamed with panic, watching the cat turn and creep stealthily towards the tree.

"*Someone get that Splint off the tree!*" barked Tree-Lord. "*Quickly! GET HIM OFF!*" But it was too late. The cat was already down at the bottom, looking inquisitively up at all the lights and Tree-Dwellers that were frantically running around the branches, trying to find somewhere to hide.

The cat placed its front paws on a lower branch and casually lifted itself into the tree. Tree-Lord screamed down to his lights, "*Get that blasted cat away...! GET IT OFF!*"

Immediately the lights began springing out of their sockets and jumping from all angles down at the invasive cat, like a swarm of bees. The cat flinched and hissed wildly from the painful shocks, while sparks showered down everywhere.

In extreme pain, Splint climbed to his feet and desperately clambered up through the branches. The cat noticed him and lashed out a paw, but could not reach him, as wave after wave of stinging Army-Lights continued their attack.

After lashing out at the lights, the cat quickly climbed up through the lower branches of the tree, trying to get to Splint, and also trying to find some shelter from the stinging Army-Lights.

Splint was exhausted, terrified and in pain, but he desperately needed to stay one step ahead of the cat.

The cat simply could not get away from the attacking lights that were bombarding it from every angle, and briefly turned its attention back to them. It swatted several of them out of the air with an outstretched paw and they exploded into hundreds of sparkling pieces. The cat hissed and twitched as the next barrage of lights cascaded down upon it.

Splint lost his footing on a branch and slipped, falling back on to a lower one. He landed with one of his legs dangling through the needles of the branch, in full view of the cat.

The cat, shaking the tree violently with its weight, reached up to grab onto Splint's exposed leg, but Splint managed to lift it just ahead of the cat's swing and barely scrambled away with his life.

Near the top, Tree-Lord had felt the tree's violent shake. "What's happening down there? I can't see what's going on, darn it!" He now feared for his own safety and turned to the lights still holding Larry and Debbie. "Go on, then! What are you waiting for? Go and get that pesky cat off the tree, for goodness sake! *Go on, get it!*"

The lights just stood there. "*What are you gawking at?*" yelled Tree-Lord. "*Get down there, you imbeciles!*"

The lights released them, and Larry grabbed Debbie in his arms. She started to wake up.

"Are you okay?" asked Larry.

"Uh... Yes, I'm fine, I think."

"Come on, let's get you somewhere safe!" Larry lifted her up in his arms, then jumped down a few branches, and away from Tree-Lord.

"You two won't be going anywhere once I've dealt with that *cat!*" scowled Tree-Lord. The tree shook and swayed again from side to side, and Tree-Lord realized he was now on his own up there.

Further down, Splint was still struggling to keep away from the incessant reaches of the cat. A new wave of lights jumped down to attack the intruder, and it lashed out in all directions, shaking the tree even more. It hissed and clawed at the lights as they shot down at it, like guided missiles, smashing into its body in an explosion of sparks and small fires.

The Tree-Dwellers were screaming with panic, running in all directions to get out of the way of the oncoming cat and all the projectile lights.

Looking down into the tree, Larry could see the cat was closing in fast on Splint, who was desperately struggling to pull himself up onto another branch.

"*Come on, Splint! You can do it!*" Larry yelled. "*Keep going and don't look down!*" Larry could see Splint was too exhausted and was now just trying to cling onto anything. "Debbie, hold onto a strong branch and stay here! I'm going for Splint!"

She nodded with concern and tightly grabbed a thick branch an instant before the whole tree shook violently again, causing a couple of dwellers above to fall helplessly past her, down into the dense branches below.

Larry jumped as quickly as he could down through the branches. He passed his Bedtime-Branch and noticed his trusted

umbrella still hanging there. He quickly
grabbed it then dropped down several
branches to arrive just above Splint.

Lying on his stomach, Larry
pushed his arm through the branch
towards Splint. *"Grab my hand
Splint...! Grab it!"* yelled Larry.

With the cat this close, seeing it lash out
with its huge razor sharp claws, Larry realized
just how big and vicious this thing really
was. Branches cracked and split all
around under the power and weight of
the cat, as the few lights left kept up their
futile attack.

*"Come on, Splint, you can do
it...!"* screamed Larry, pushing his arm and shoulder as far down
through the branch as he could. *"Come on, grab my hand!"*

Splint glanced up with a look of sheer desperation on his
face, and with every ounce of strength he could muster, lunged out at
Larry's hand.

Just as Splint felt the ends of Larry's fingers, the cat jumped
up and its claws grabbed onto Splint's back, ripping him violently
from Larry.

"NO!" screamed Larry, watching Splint getting helplessly
tossed down through the branches into the darkness.

In grabbing Splint, the cat lost its balance too and slipped,
falling backwards down through the tree. It desperately clawed at the
passing branches, snapping them like thin twigs. Nothing could hold

its sheer weight and it continued to tumble. The cat fell through the lighting cable, which in turn pulled on the branches the cable was lying across.

As it was pulled down, the cable released branch after branch, whipping each one back like catapults, throwing helpless dwellers all around the tree like rubber bands.

Debbie heard a strange *'twang'* sound above her head and glanced up to see the lighting cable slip off a branch and whip down towards her. It flicked her violently off the branch and down through the tree. She screamed, falling helplessly towards the thrashing cat below.

Splint was trying to get up from where he had been thrown by the cat, and at the very last minute, managed to duck in time to see the cable whip past his head, missing him by the thickness of a pine needle.

Debbie grabbed at the cable, just as it caught hold of a branch and abruptly stopped, yanking her shoulder hard. She glanced down to see that she was swinging within reach of the thrashing cat. She screamed, *"HELP! LARRY, HELP...!"* The cat was not just struggling with the Army-Lights, it was becoming increasingly tangled amongst the wires too, causing the tree to swing even more erratically.

Tree-Lord, still helplessly stuck in his wiring at the top of the tree, was unsure as to what was happening down below. He had no lights to inform him and could just see some sparking under the thick branches from the lights' attack on the cat, and dwellers, aimlessly running from branch to branch.

Suddenly he felt the cable, and himself, being pulled. It was the weight of the cat. He tried grabbing onto the branches around him with his arms. *"No…! What's going on down there? No…! No, I won't…! Nooo!"* A look of shock and desperation appeared on Tree-Lord's face, as he felt the pine needles begin to rip from the branches one by one into his hand, causing his grip to falter.

Down in the tree, Debbie also felt her fingers slipping from the cable. There was another shake of the tree and her fingers slipped off, and she screamed, falling helplessly into the path of the cat.

Larry jumped from a branch and latched himself onto another with his trusted umbrella. He swung across her path not a moment too soon and grabbed her arm, pulling her away to safety.

More branches flicked away from the cable, and the cat fell again, swinging the tree alarmingly to one side. It jolted to a stop and everyone screamed, as the last few lights finished themselves off on the invasive cat.

Tree-Lord looked around in a panic as the tree creaked and swung violently to the other side, hitting the wall with great force, before stopping for a moment.

"NO, I WON'T LET IT… NO! COME ON, SOMEONE HELP ME!" panicked Tree-Lord. Without warning, the tree gave a strange *'creak!'*, then a loud *'crack!'* sound, which shocked Tree-Lord into silence, as he knew what was about to happen.

Down below, Larry tried yelling above the screams and chaos. *"Hold on tight, everyone! The tree… I think it's going to… ahhhh…!"*

The top of the tree began sliding down the wall, cracking loudly as it went. Larry and Debbie held on tightly as other less fortunate dwellers lost their grip and fell helplessly down towards the ground.

Tree-Lord tried without success to pull himself out of the socket he had been locked into all of these years. Sitting there helplessly screaming at his Army-Lights, he felt himself being dragged away with the falling tree.

As the side of the tree met the ground, the top, where Tree-Lord had been perched, whipped down and smashed him on the edge of the wooden coffee table.

Tree-Lord was smashed into a million pieces and sparks flew around the room, setting off a couple of short-lived fires on the carpet.

The branches of the tree finally settled, and the room dropped into a dark silence.

XXIV

Picking Up The Pieces

VOICES WERE HEARD UNDER THE TREE and branches began to move, as the Tree-Dwellers struggled out from under them. Shocked and dazed, they began searching for their family and friends.

Larry lifted a hand up through a thick pine branch and pushed it off him. "Ohhh…! Now that *did* hurt!" he sighed, turning to Debbie, who had curled up into a small ball under his arm. "Hey, Debbie. Are you okay?" and gently lifted her head.

She slowly opened her eyes. "Yes, I'm fine, I think," and she sat up. "How are you? How's that foot of yours…?"

"Oh…!" smiled Larry, looking down at it. "Yeah, it's fine. I think it'll be okay," he said as they gently helped one another to their feet.

Tinsel ran over, barking and wagging his tail at them, then loyally wrapped himself again around Larry's foot. "No wonder you don't like cats, boy!" chuckled Larry, looking around at all the mess.

"*Where's Splint?*" asked Debbie anxiously. "Did you see him?"

"No, not after he was thrown down into the tree by the cat," replied Larry.

They both looked eagerly around, fearing the worst.

"So where is he?" asked Debbie, getting more concerned.

"*Has anyone seen Splint...?*" called Larry.

"Who?" replied Max, from a few branches away.

"*Oh, come on, Max...!*" begged Larry, shaking his head. "Now let's not start that again!"

"Oh, Splint...! Haven't seen him at all!" replied Max, helping Dan out from under a branch. "Sorry, Larry... not since we were up in the tree. But I tell you, he's a tough one, that's for sure." He took off his cap to scratch his head. "The way he took that cat on... what a hero, I say! As a matter of fact, you all are!"

"Thanks, Max...! Are you two okay?"

"Oh, yeah Larry, course we are. It'll takes more than the odd cat to put us down," chuckled Dan, brushing himself off.

From the corner of her eye, Debbie noticed a familiar foot poking out from under a branch. It was next to a dying Army-Light that was still buzzing around on the ground. "*Splint...! Splint...! Are you okay?*"

Larry and Debbie jumped around the light and over to Splint. Larry quickly and carefully pulled away the heavy branch.

"*Ohhh...!*" moaned Splint, lying in a curled up heap on the ground, with pine needles and bits of wood scattered all over him. "Are we there yet...?" he murmured, trying to imitate Larry back at the stairs, while struggling to keep a straight face.

"You two... What are you both like!" laughed Larry, carefully helping Splint to his feet.

"*Ouuuch!*" yelped Splint, and looking down he noticed one of his wooden legs had been badly split. "Ooh, now that's a nasty nick, eh?"

"Yes, it looks painful, Splint. Are you sure you're okay?" asked Debbie.

"Yeah, I'll be fine," answered Splint, and he looked around at all the carnage. "Wow...! Now *that... that's* what I call a rush!" and paused a moment. "So what happened? I don't really remember..."

Larry began to explain. "The cat—"

"*Ugh! Yeah, the cat! Where is it?*" interrupted Splint, looking anxiously around for signs of it.

"She's under here!" replied Max, as Dan lifted up a branch to expose the cat's tail, which was still wrapped in the wiring.

"She's twitching like you wouldn't believe under 'ere!" laughed Dan. "She'll be okay though, but I doubt she'll be coming anywhere near the tree from now on, methinks...! Will she, Max?"

"Never a truer word spoken, me ole-mucker," nodded Max, slapping Dan on the back. The slap caused Dan to lose his grip on the branch and it flicked down, whipping the cat, causing it to flinch and whine.

"Sorry!" grinned Max cheekily.

Splint, breathing a sigh of relief, looked to Larry and Debbie. "So what does Tree-Lord have to say about his *'protective'* Army-

Lights now…?" He took a closer look at his injured leg.

"Actually Splint, it was *all* Tree-Lord's doing," explained Larry.

"What… what do you mean?"

"He had my brother killed," continued Larry, gazing out at the mess in the room, "and goodness knows how many others over the years."

"*What…?* B… But, why would he do that?" asked Splint, looking totally shocked and confused.

Larry quickly glanced at Debbie, then back to Splint. "He just couldn't deal with anyone else getting the family's attention."

"What! Attention? All this was… *jealousy?*" said Splint, shaking his head in disbelief. "He did it because he was *jealous?*" He glanced around at the split branches and broken lights that littered the floor. "So where is he now?"

"He's gone. We saw him fall against the coffee table," answered Debbie. "There isn't anything left of him."

"Wow. What a way to go, hey!" said Splint, before drifting away into his own thoughts. He wondered if Tree-Lord could have had anything to do with the disappearance of his own brothers. But how could he? Tree-Lord was never in the shop when Splint was there, either before or after his brothers disappeared.

Splint smiled bravely back at Debbie and Larry. He knew in his heart that he was no closer to finding his own brothers now, than he was when he was back in the bargain basket at the shop.

"Splint," said Larry, clearing his throat. "I didn't get a chance to say it earlier, but I'm really sorry too… about your brothers, that is." He placed a hand on his shoulder. "Debbie told me… I'm really sorry. I wish we had answers for you here."

Splint nodded. "Thanks, Larry. Maybe I'll never know..."

Debbie glanced at Larry, then smiled affectionately back at Splint. "But you know you have us two now, don't you...?"

Tinsel barked up at them.

"Sorry... three!" smiled Debbie. "And you have a whole new family here on the tree, if you like? We'd all love to have you stay with us!"

Splint paused, thinking for a moment, before a smile wiped across his face. "Really...?"

Larry and Debbie both nodded.

"Yeah... I do, don't I," smiled Splint, and looked over at the Tree-Dwellers who were quickly approaching, wanting to be the first to welcome them all back as heroes.

For the first time in a very long time, Splint felt like he belonged somewhere. Wherever his brothers were and whatever they were doing, they were always with him in his heart, along with the rest of his new family on the wonderful, great big magical Christmas tree.

Suddenly, the hallway door rattled and the door slowly swung open.

"Burglars...? I don't know! I haven't got x-ray vision, have I!?" whispered a voice nervously from the hallway. "Now, stand back...!"

The living room light switched on and Dad burst in, yelling at the top of his lungs, with a garden spade over his shoulder, ready to swing. He anxiously looked around to see who was there, but he only noticed the fallen tree, the scattered decorations and the broken tree lights that littered the floor.

"What the heck happened here...?" mumbled Dad as bits of glass from the lights cracked under his slippers.

"Oh my goodness, *the tree...!*" gasped Mom, poking her head from behind the door.

"Stand back, love!" warned Dad, pulling up his pajama bottoms. "There's glass all over the place here!" and carefully bent over to lift the tree back up.

The cat jumped out from underneath the branches, still wrapped in the wiring and twitching uncontrollably. It startled Dad into dropping the tree and he jumped back, ready to swing the garden spade.

"*Ooh!* That flipping cat..." sighed Dad angrily. "*Ohhh...!* How many times have I told it to stay away from that tree? If I've told it once, I've told it a *thousand times!* Right, next year we make sure it's *not* getting into this room at night. I mean anything could have happened." A couple of sparks from a broken light skipped out across the floor.

"But we unplugged the lights, didn't we?" asked Mom, looking rather puzzled. She watched the twitching cat scurry away into the dining room, still struggling to untangle itself from the wiring.

"Yeah, I'm sure we did," answered Dad, looking equally as puzzled. He picked up the cable off the floor and followed it to the plug, where he noticed it was unplugged from the wall socket.

"Uh…! Now that's weird!" sighed Dad, pulling his pajamas up again. "And why did all the lights pop out of their sockets? How could *that* have happened…?"

"Oh, I don't know," sighed Mom. "Come on, it's late. We have a really long drive ahead of us tomorrow. Come on back to bed," then yawned, "Let's just make sure it's unplugged and we'll clear it all up in the morning."

"Yeah, I never really did like those lights, especially that big one we put near the top," said Dad, dropping the cable. "It never sat well with me. Where did we get them again? Wasn't it from your Auntie or something?" He switched off the room lights.

"No," whispered Mom, quietly climbing the stairs back to bed. "Those were left here by the last owners when we bought the house. Don't you remember?"

"Oh yeah, that's right," agreed Dad, closing the hallway door behind him. "Anyway it's new ones next year. We can't have lights popping out of their sockets like that, something dangerous could happen." Their voices faded up the stairs.

Early the next morning, just before daybreak, the tree ornaments were being carefully packed back in the Christmas box.

"I can't believe that every tree light was smashed!" laughed Dad, shaking his head. "Though a few of the ornaments *did* get a bit of a beating when the tree fell, I've got to say…"

"Sorry, what's that, love? I wasn't quite listening," asked Mom, quickly walking past him into the hallway.

"Aaron…! Emma…! Are you both packed and ready up there?" called Mom up the stairs. *"We're leaving in a minute! Oh, and have you both cleaned your teeth?"* She climbed the stairs to check on them both.

"Oh, which reminds me!" mumbled Dad, walking away from the box and back into the kitchen.

Debbie and Larry had just been placed back in the box, side by side. They turned to one another and she acted out *'the kiss'* to Larry. She smiled, watching it invisibly flutter over to him and *'smack!'* hit him right in the face, nudging the whole box.

They both smiled and turned back into their solid form, just as Dad returned from the kitchen, holding something in his hand.

"Ah…! There you go little guy. A bit of paint and glue sorted you out as well, just like our little snowman in there," said Dad, smiling. "I still can't believe we found the piece of that foot amongst all the glass on the floor. Anyway you're all sorted now," and he lowered Splint into the last spot in the box, padded with soft tissue paper.

Dad reached over for the lid and began to close it down on top of the box. As he did so, Debbie and Larry looked over and smiled at Splint, who smiled back.

The lid closed, and was then quickly opened again. Larry, Debbie and Splint were all sleeping in their solid state.

"Huh...!" said Dad, sounding confused. "I could have sworn..." then laughed, "No...!" and closed up, for another year, the 'Secrets of a Christmas Box'.

A Note From The Author

Growing out of my childhood, I remembered trying to hold onto those magical feelings I only got at Christmas time, the warm fuzziness in my stomach and the giddy excitement of knowing Santa Claus would soon be arriving.

But those feelings faded and in their place completely new ones developed. Equally as good mind you, just different.

So I wanted to create a world that captured those magical feelings I had as a child, but also include a sense of what Christmas means to me today, every time I open up that wonderful Christmas box.

Acknowledgments

I wish to express my sincere gratitude to:

Those who read drafts of the manuscript. Thank you Bob Davies, Richard Thompson, Kasi Dodge, Malous Kossarian, Israel Havran, and Chris Kirshbaum, for your interest and good judgment.

To Judy Reveal, who guided me through the first draft. I learned so much from you, and miss those long phone calls.

Thank you Spike, for your character and unquestioned loyalty. I hope it is given justice through the pages of this book.

Thank you Azam Sadat, for the hundreds of wonderful sacks you painstakingly handmade.

To my good friend Micheál Kiely, for your encouragement and steady council that helped me stay the course.

To Golriz, my partner and soul mate. Thank you for your inspiration, your guidance and support. For being with me all the way, and for just being you.

And a special thanks to my parents; for help in making me who I am and for giving me all those wonderful Christmases.